I0566687

Sweet Ruin

University of Branton

Nazarea Andrews

Sweet Ruin

This book is a work of fiction. Names, characters, places, and incidents are either products of the author's imagination or are used fictitiously. Any resemblance to actual persons, living or dead, business establishments, events, or locales is entirely coincidental. The author makes no claims to, but instead acknowledges the trademarked status and trademark owners of any wordmarks mentioned in this work of fiction including brands or products.

Copyright © 2014 by Nazarea Andrews.

Sweet Ruin by Nazarea Andrews
All rights reserved. Published in the United States of America by A&A Literary.

Summary: Megan Beauchamp has been running from expectations--and Branton--but when Asher and Luca convince her to go on a road trip back home, all three have to reevaluate what they want--and what they're willing to sacrifice for each other.

ISBN: 978-0-9894799-4-3
1. New Adult. 2. Romance. 3. Hollywood.

No part of this book may be used or reproduced in any manner whatsoever without written permission, except in the case of brief quotations embodied in critical articles and reviews.

For information, address 14207 Ridge Court, Upatoi GA 31829.
www.nazareaandrews.com

Edited by Rachel Bateman
Cover design by Melissa Stevens of The Illustrated Author
Cover art copyright©: Nazarea Andrews
Ebook Formatting by Ink in Motion
Paperback Formatting by Ink in Motion

It's good to be on top…

Asher Knox has it all. Girls, wealth, a career most would kill for. He's just landed the biggest job of his career. And he's miserable.

She's fighting her way from the bottom…

Megan Beauchamp has no illusions about why she was chosen to be Asher's PA. She's pretty, and down to earth, and everything the Hollywood star always falls for. Too bad Megan is just paying her dues and has no interest in anything but advancing at her PR firm.

He'll throw it all away…

Luca James knows what he wants. And he's waited a long time for the window to open—when it does, he'll walk away from the career he's built for a chance at something real.

When Megan's boss threatens to fire her, Luca and Asher convince her to leave town with them. Between bad hotels and pit stop confessionals, the three are drawn closer together. And the lines blur even more in Branton, where Megan is forced to look at everything she left behind.

But they want more, and Megan will be forced to choose between the men she loves and the life she thought she wanted. And in a town like Branton, the secrets she keeps won't be hidden for long.

Books by Nazarea Andrews

Edge of the Falls

University of Branton
This Love
Beautiful Broken
Sweet Ruin
Fractured Perfection (Oct 2014)

The World Without End
The World Without a Future
The Endless Horde (Dec 2014)

Girl Lost (May 2014)

With Aj Elmore:
Prince of Blood and Steel

Sweet Ruin

University of Branton

Nazarea Andrews

Sweet Ruin

Chapter One

Megan

It's New Year's Eve. I'm surrounded by people, at the biggest party in LA. Tomorrow, it's all anyone will talk about, and I will be able to say *I was there.*

Of course, I'm working.

I slide through the crowd of people, past pretty girls hanging on this year's hottest actors and biggest singers. Well. Not the *hottest* actor. Everyone is wondering where Asher Knox is—whispers that will become barely controlled shouts if the broody star doesn't get his shit together soon.

My lips compress, and I fake a smile as I make my way through the massive crowd.

There it is. The door to the stairwell. I angle toward it, exchanging greetings with a few lower-tier actors and an independent director as I make my way to the exit. As soon as the door slams shut behind me, I breathe a sigh of relief. I love crowds and parties, but sometimes I just need a dark, quiet stairwell.

A door bangs shut above me, and I hear a disgruntled girl muttering, "Bastard."

I smile—found him.

I hurry up the stairs, the sequins on my green dress throwing the light. An actress in a popular TV drama meets me coming down, her lips twisted. Even angry and frowning, she's gorgeous. "Save yourself a headache, darling. He's in no mood for company."

I grin. "I'm not company."

Her eyebrows go up, but she does nothing else to dissuade me, and I hurry up the last flight of stairs.

I take a deep breath, smoothing down my cocktail dress and tucking my hair behind my ears. Then I open the door and step out onto the roof.

He doesn't flinch at my intrusion, and I have a few heartbeats to take him in. The wide shoulders and narrow waist flowing into long legs, the thin fingers that wrap around the bannister. Thick, shaggy black hair that is in desperate need of a haircut. The suit that cost more money than I like to think about, his coat now discarded on a dirty folding chair.

Even here, despondent and hiding from the public, Asher Knox is the most attractive man I've ever met.

"Come look," he says, and I shiver.

Asher twists at the waist, million dollar smile lit by the city lights and gilded silver by the moon. "Come on, Megs. Just for a minute—look, and then you can lecture and I'll go down to be a good boy."

His accent is thicker. I frown—he usually hides that, as much as he can. But there's something pleading in his crystal blue gaze, and it's the closest I'm going to get to a win tonight, so I take a step forward. "Promise?"

He grins, and I relax, walking the rest of the way across the roof. He turns back to the view. I take a place at his side, with a few inches between us. His eyes flick down to the space then up to me. He smirks. I give him my best scolding look, and he laughs soundlessly as he turns to face the city.

He's right. It's gorgeous, the sparkling lights of the city a sea of light backdropped by the moon. I can almost understand why he is drawn to it.

"You know, I never went to parties, back home. We did a quiet night in for New Year's. Tournaments on the Xbox and such."

"Asher," I say, trying hard to keep the exasperation out of my voice. "This is what you worked for. Enjoy it. Or at least pretend."

He sighs, tipping his head back, staring at the night sky. Desolation plays across his features—broody is what the papers call him, dark. Difficult is what his directors and co-stars are saying.

And brilliant. Effortless.

They don't know the half of it.

I take a deep breath and reach for his arm.

Asher

I stare at the tiny fingers wrapped around my wrist and, absurdly, wish I'd discarded my shirt along with my jacket.

Megan hasn't touched me in three weeks. Three weeks, four days. It was closer to a month, before that. She is very careful with these little touches, dishing them out like pieces of gold. I've learned I can never tell when one is coming. They always hit at the most unexpected time.

Sometimes, I think half the stunts I pull are just to see if I can goad her into touching me. Like this—retreating. I like the solitude, of course. Much more than the craziness that is downstairs. But if I'm very honest—which I'm not, not often—I knew she would chase me up here. It's her job, to make sure I face the adoring public.

"Look. Come downstairs. Smile and talk to some directors. Get your picture taken a few times. As soon as the ball drops, we'll get out of here. Can you do that for me?"

Of course. There isn't really a question. "What do I get out of it?"

She huffs, a noise that is half laugh, half exasperation. "A quiet weekend. I won't even make you leave the house to eat."

I arch an eyebrow, twisting to stare at her. "Promise."

Megs smirks, but nods. I glance away, staring out at the sea of lights, and the dark sky brightened by them.

I always thought I wanted this. It's a long way from England. And I love my work—when I get to focus on that. It's when the other shit intrudes—the press and constant barrage of questions about my personal life, my manger trying to navigate me where I don't want to go. That's what I don't love. That's when I want nothing but the quiet of the nearest rooftop.

"Knox," she says, her voice crisp and demanding.

I glance at her briefly. In a sea of blonde models and brunette beauties, she stands out with wild red curls and a smattering of freckles her makeup doesn't quite cover. She's all fiery hair and peaches and cream skin, and no-nonsense practicality that reminds me of home.

I shake that thought, along with the longing for quiet, and summon the playboy smile—slightly crooked and self-assured. I grab my suit coat from the chair and stroll to the door to the roof.

I glance back when I open it, and she's still standing there, watching me. In moments like this, I see more than professional concern—I see worry and the hint of caring she's so careful to hide. I swallow hard and grin. "Come on, darling."

Luca

Megan doesn't know I'm here. She's good at ignoring things not immediately in her line of sight when she's working. And since she dragged Asher downstairs, he's been swarmed by people anxious for his attention.

"Are you going to talk to him?" Sun asks, leaning against the bar by my elbow.

"Why?" I ask, twisting the glass of champagne in my hand.

"Because you want to. Because you'll be working with him on *Black Tides*. Because your best friend is standing next to him, and it gives you an in."

I roll my eyes. "I don't want an in."

Sun is quiet for a long moment, then she laughs, a soft noise. "Luca, you've been waiting for an in for almost two years."

I don't respond, and she curses softly before walking away.

Megan and Asher are moving through the room, flashbulbs marking their passage.

I want to be there, with them. I want to be the arm Megan is leaning against. I don't have time for this, not right now—Megan is working, and Asher barely knows I exist. I should leave. Before I end up doing something I'll regret.

I text Sun—easier than trying to find her.

Me: Going to go home. If you talk to Meg, give her my love.

Sun: Is that all you want me to give her? ;)

I swallow a laugh and turn away.

Asher Knox is standing there, hands thrust deep into the pockets of his suit pants, a blank expression on his face.

"Sorry," I murmur. His eyes spark with interest, and he offers me a shade of that famous smile.

"No worries, mate."

I step to one side, and Asher eases onto a bar stool. "Can I get a beer?" he asks, quietly. The bartender responds immediately. I laugh.

Knox slides a quick look at me. "What?"

"I waited almost thirty minutes for a glass of champagne."

He looks uncomfortable. But then, Asher hates being recognized, even when he puts himself in a situation where being recognized is inevitable.

"Do you want anything?" he asks, instead of addressing the discomfort.

"No," I say. I swallow dryly.

"Luca?" a startled, sweet voice says.

Both of us turn, and Asher looks quickly at me. "What are you doing here?" Megan asks, a smile on her lips. She leans in to give me a quick hug, and I brush a kiss across her cheek.

"Sun wanted to come. I had the tickets. I'm actually headed out soon," I say. Asher shifts, and I focus on him. "Luca James," I say, extending a hand.

He looks confused as he shakes it briefly. "Asher Knox."

I grin. "Yeah. I know."

"Asher, Luca is one of my best friends. I didn't realize he'd be here tonight."

There's a hint of censure in her tone, something that tells me she isn't happy—but then, Megan hates mixing business and pleasure. "Like I said, I'm on my way out. We still getting together later this week?"

She nods, and I give Asher a nod, trying to keep my face bland. As I walk away, I can feel them watching me and hear his softly murmured question.

I try very hard to think about anything but the fact that I don't want to leave them.

Chapter Two

Megan

I wake up with a pounding headache and a mouth that feels fuzzy with the taste of stale alcohol. Somewhere in the apartment, my phone is warbling, an awful song Nik programed last time she came to town that I haven't bothered to change. I fall out of bed and limp on one heel down the hall. I fish my phone from my purse and slump against the wall, ignoring my pounding head as I answer. "Do you have any idea what time it is?"

"Where is he?" my boss demands, ignoring the rasp of my voice.

I roll my eyes. "He's in bed. Where anyone who was at that party last night would be."

If Kevin catches the dig, he ignores it. "Get your ass moving, girl."

"Why?" I come alert and reach down to tug my shoe off before hurrying down the hall. Scenarios of everything that could have gone wrong play through my head.

"Because if you leave him alone too long, he goes off the reservation, and I don't have time to track him down again. I need you to keep him leashed until next week."

"Don't worry so much," I say. "I know how to do my job. I'll keep him quiet until the call back."

"Has he agreed to take it if they offer?"

I sigh, reaching in to turn on my shower. "He's deciding. He waffles, you know that. Until an offer is on the table, he won't make a decision. I'm putting the pressure on him, though, and it seems to be working."

"Well, get him to commit. That's why you're there."

I bark a laugh. "I'm here because I'm the type of girl he likes to fuck."

"Whatever," my uncle says, brusquely. "Keep him in sight and out of trouble until we have the contract."

I take a deep breath. "After that he needs a break."

"Megan, we've discussed this," Kevin starts, and I jump in to cut him off.

"I know. Taking him out of the spotlight could backfire. But if we leave him in the pressure for too long, he'll go off on his own, and we can't control that. If we offer the escape, we call the shots."

"He'll know what we're doing."

Of course he will. Knox is a lot of things—difficult, sexy, brooding, and unpredictable—but he is also brilliant and almost always knows when I'm manipulating him. Doesn't mean I can't do it. I've been his personal assistant—a glorified babysitter—for longer than any of my predecessors, precisely because I *can* manipulate him.

"He won't care," I say.

Kevin is quiet for almost ten seconds. Long enough I check my phone to make sure he hasn't hung up. Then, "Fine. We'll talk about it in a few days. Get him through the call back."

"Yes, sir."

I hang up and strip out of my cocktail dress, stepping into the still lukewarm shower. I don't have time to wait for it to heat.

Kevin is right—leaving Knox by himself is a recipe for disaster.

I pull up to the house and stare at it while I sip my coffee. It's dark, but the curtains in the living room are moving—which means Knox left the back door open again. I curse and kick off my heels, sliding into a pair of flip flops I keep for occasions like this. I grab my coffee and the large hot tea and slip out of the car, nudging the door shut with my butt before making my way around the side of the house and out onto the private beach. It's empty, the early morning light watery and cold as the waves lap at the shore. I shiver, staring. I love the ocean—it's one of the perks of working as Asher Knox's PA. I love how small and unimportant I feel staring at it.

I shake off the fanciful thoughts and make my way down the windy beach. There's a small natural curve, a rock wall rising up to brace the tiny cove from the wind. It's Knox's favorite place to go—nine times out of ten, I find him there. True to form, he's sitting in the sand, arms looped around his knees as he stares at the water. I approach and perch on the Adirondack chair he dragged out here for me.

He doesn't stir as I sit, but takes the cup when I tap his shoulder with it.

We don't talk. My head hurts too much to bother, and he likes the morning quiet.

Despite growing up in London and moving to Hollywood three years ago at the age of twenty-one, Asher is still remarkably outdoorsy. It's annoying as hell—there have been several occasions one of his PAs would show up and find the house deserted, Asher gone.

Going off the grid without his cell phone is one of his favorite pastimes. He always turns up, usually within a week. Smelly and covered in bug bites and peaceful. For a while, his moodiness lightened.

It never lasts, though.

I shiver, and he glances back at me. I'm annoyed he's in a worn pair of blue jeans, shirtless and barefoot, while I'm in leggings and a thick, long sweater dress. But he looks good. Sleepy and content.

"Did I earn a reprieve?" he asks, gently teasing.

I snort, and he laughs soundlessly. "Don't you get bored with the quiet?" I ask. He looks faintly horrified.

"No! Don't you ever get exhausted with all the noise?"

Yes. Of course. But I thrive on it.

I don't say that—don't answer his question. "Quiet weekend. I'll even go to the store—if you promise not to vanish while I'm gone."

He looks away. "Where would I go?" he asks, his tone bitter. I pull back, surprised. "Every time I leave the house, I'm mobbed."

"Most actors wouldn't complain about that, Ash." Most actors would give their right ball to be in his position—being the face of a cult phenomenon is nothing to sneer at, and making it to the big screen after the TV series wrapped was just the icing on the cake.

He smirks. "I'm not most actors."

I bite down on my response, choking the sarcasm off before I can snap at him.

He rolls to his feet with unconscious grace, brushing sand from his hands. He looks, in this moment, like a young god.

"Come on, Megs. I'll cook for you. Nobody has to go anywhere for a while."

It's a tempting offer—who knew Asher Knox would turn out to be a better cook than I am? "Real bacon? Not that turkey shit."

His lips curl into that infuriatingly sexy smirk, and he extends a hand to pull me to my feet.

Asher

She doesn't take it. She never does. But she does rise and pads barefoot next to me toward the house. I resist the urge to stare at her—I make an effort to not be too blatant. She appreciates it. The first week Kevin had Megan assigned to me, I wasn't so circumspect. I was obvious and over the top—everything that I had used on other girls to get them into bed.

It didn't impress Megan. She'd tolerated it for a few days then abruptly quit.

I'd been reeling and stormed into Kevin's office, demanding her back.

She agreed—on her own terms. Romantic relationships are firmly out of bounds. I know that—and because I need her calm steady presence more than I want to fuck her, I tolerate her asinine rules.

It doesn't mean I don't want her. I like to remind her that we both know where I stand on that.

She leans against the side of the house, brushing sand from her feet before stepping inside. The kitchen is quiet and dark—the way she likes it after a night out. I can see the tension lines around her eyes and the stubborn set of her mouth. I wonder again about the young man at the bar, the one who watched her with too-hungry eyes. I'm tempted to ask, but it's pointless.

"Catch," I say, and her hands come up to snatch the bottle of Tylenol out of the air. She gives me a weak smile and pops two before curling into a chair at the table, her legs tucked under her. She props one hand in her hair, scrolling through the news on her tablet.

When she's like this, it's easy to see the girl fresh from college, fighting her way up the ranks of a cutthroat talent agency. It's easy to see she's just as young and scared as I feel. It's easy to see her vulnerabilities.

She doesn't let this side show often.

"Your staring, Knox," she says, her voice tart. I laugh, and her green eyes dart up, locking with mine. Amused warning.

Duly noted. I twist away, going to the fridge to gather the makings for breakfast. I start a pot of coffee for Megan as the griddle heats, and then drop a few slices of bacon into the pan.

"What are the vultures saying today?"

"There's a few pictures of you and Ashley Moore."

I make a face. The studio likes seeing us together—and we make a pretty picture. But the girl grates my nerves. Probably, sleeping with her was a bad idea. In all fairness, she had that girl next door innocence down pat.

I grin. Until I got her naked in my hotel room. Then all her expertise came pouring out. The things that woman could do with her tongue...

I shake the thought. "It wouldn't kill you to have lunch with her," Megan says.

"No." I snort. "I'm not feeding that tramp's delusions of grandeur. I wouldn't have gone near her if I knew the paps were around."

"What did I tell you?" she says, annoyed. "They're always around."

I ignore that, bringing breakfast to the table before retreating to get two glasses of juice. I return to find Megan staring at me, concern in her eyes.

"How close are you to going off the reservation?" she asks, pushing aside all pretense.

The feeling of being suffocated, the pressure of everything—the studio and my agent and Megan and my fans—all of it wells up in me suddenly. My grip on my fork tightens, and Megs glances down.

"I have a friend—back home. I think he'd be a good person for you to consult with after you take the Lafitte role."

I struggle to keep up, making the mental leap in conversations. "Why?"

"He's an expert. A professor at the college I graduated from. The gentleman pirate sorta became his life's work."

I've spent my life studying people and picking up on their ticks. And right now, I'm hearing more than a student's fondness for a professor.

"Who is he?"

Megan

Asher's question comes out low and almost menacing. Except Knox isn't menacing. He's sweet and disturbed and moodier than fucking Hamlet, but he's not menacing. I blink at him.

No. I'm not reading him wrong. That's anger in his eyes.

"Atticus Grimes—a history professor at the University of Branton."

His gaze doesn't falter.

"You need a break," I say. "So let's get through next week—they're going to offer you the role. We all know they will. We'll have about a month before filming starts. So let's get out of town."

"To go visit your professor?" he asks, his voice dark silk. I shiver, my blood spiking. Angry Knox is hot.

"You and me, a road trip to Branton. You can talk to him about the character. We can eat horribly awful food and do touristy shit and get you out of the spotlight for a while."

He's ignoring his food, staring at me like I've grown a third head. It makes me nervous, when he stares like that. I flash a smile.

"Kevin will never let me disappear for a month."

Some of the tension eases out of me, and I grin. "Oh, honey. You take the role next week, and Kevin will give you whatever you fucking want."

Interest sparks in his eyes, and I know, in that moment more than any other, that I have him.

And I'm not sure how to feel about that, because a month alone with Asher Knox is a disaster waiting to happen.

Chapter Three

Megan

"Knox is fucking insane."

I switch the phone to my other hand, propping it between my shoulder and ear as I navigate through the streets of downtown LA. I'm supposed to be off today. Kevin was taking Knox to the call back. I had planned on a quiet afternoon at my apartment, a little shopping to pick up some groceries, and meeting Luca and Sun for drinks tonight. It's been too long since I saw them, aside from that brief moment on New Year's Eve, and I was actually looking forward to a night out when I wasn't wrangling Knox.

"What do mean, Kevin? He was fine when I left last night."

"Did you put some crazy idea in his head that he could take a month off if he landed the *Black Tides* role?"

I bite back a curse. He wasn't supposed to know that shit yet. "We talked about it, remember. He needs a break."

"A break. A break, Megan, is a trip to fucking Aspen for a weekend. It's not a cross country trip in your beater."

"Then fork up the cash for something better," I snarl. "Or find someone else Asher will tolerate. I think Mandy would fit—oh wait. She got thrown out after an hour, didn't she?"

I'm being bitchy, and I don't care. Kevin is quiet on the other end of the line.

"What's it going to be, uncle? My way or should I go home now?"

"Fuck you, Megan."

I laugh, a bitter noise, and hang up.

My hands are shaking. I despise him. Sometimes, I think it's not worth it. Not worth the degrading comments and the bullshit and the way he treats me like the mailroom clerk. I know my job, and I know I'm good at it.

And it's not like anyone back home sees me as anything but the snot nosed kid Daddy took in when there was nowhere else to go.

I shove the thoughts of my uncle and hometown aside and park abruptly. I pull up Knox's number and text him.

Me: What's wrong? K said you were freaking out.

Knox: Where are you?

Me: Day off, remember? Do you need me?

I hold my breath waiting on his answer. I want my day off. I can already hear Sun's bitching if I cancel. But if he needs me, there isn't even an option.

Knox: I'm fine. Enjoy your day, Megs.

I stare at it. There are no emoticons—I don't think Knox even knows what they are. It's too dry, too hard to read. I hesitate, torn between wanting to call and wanting to accept his words at face value.

My phone dings, startling me, and I read the message.

Knox: Promise, Meggy. Have fun. I'll text after the call back.

I let out my breath and smile.

While I'm still thinking, I write a quick email.

To: atticus.grimes@Branton.edu
From: MegPA90@gmail.com
Subject: Huge Favor

Hey brother man.

Can I still call you that? I haven't emailed since the divorce was finalized—sorry about that. Uncle Kevin has me super busy.

That's actually why I'm writing now. I'm headed back to your neck of the woods with a client—I was wondering if you could maybe talk to him about Jean Lafitte. I can't give you much more than that over email, but if you'd like to contact me, my number hasn't changed. And if you're totally busy, I get it. Maybe we can grab coffee when I'm in town. Believe it or not, some of us miss you.

Okay, that's it.
Meg*

I hit send before I can rethink it. As I slide out of the car and slip my sunglasses on, I let myself consider that Nik is going to be furious.

The thought makes me smile.

Later that night, I'm sitting crammed between Sun and Luca at a noisy bar. Luca is eyeing the pretty blonde girl leaning over the bar, her little ass peeking out the bottom of her dress. He's almost drooling.

Actually, Sun is eyeing the same girl.

"Quit undressing her with your mind, you pervs," I order, catching the eye of our waitress. I make a circular motion, and she nods.

"Thong?" Luca guesses, still watching Blondie.

"Ten bucks says she's not wearing underwear," Sun shoots back, licking her lips.

Oh sweet lord. "You two are not," I say, lifting up a hand. "No. We're out for fun."

Sun turns wide brown eyes on me, her expression full of false innocence. "Oh, sugar, we'll have so much fun."

Luca laughs on the other side of me, a silent rumble that shakes my body.

"I'm not watching you two seduce the tourists," I say flatly.

Luca leans in, lips whispering over my pulse point. "We could seduce you, lovely girl."

I smirk, shaking my head. "I've lived with you. I've seen you work this line on too many girls to fall for it."

Sun pouts, leaning into me. I pat her arm then point at the waitress, approaching with a fresh round of shots. "Look. Tequila!"

Sun squeals happily and leans forward, bouncing in her seat.

As they flirt with the waitress, I sneak a glance at my phone. Nothing from Knox. I'm starting to worry a little.

"Phone down, lovely girl," Luca purrs in my ear. I shiver and drop it into my bra.

Luca and Sun are the first friends I made in LA when I arrived eighteen months ago, fresh from college and eager to make my mark. Kevin slammed the door in my face—and Luca was there to catch me. An indie actor, he'd been at the office when Kevin turned me away. He'd taken pity on me—in retrospect, he probably thought he could get me in bed.

And Luca is sexy enough for it. Skin the color of midnight, a shaved skull, and eyes deep enough to drown in—and the body of a fucking athlete—the boy has sex appeal in spades. It keeps him in cash when he isn't acting—there is always someone willing to pay him to stand around and look sexy in their clothes.

Going to bed with him would have been a done deal, if it weren't for his particular brand of kink.

Sun and Luca aren't a couple. They are best friends and fight like cats and dogs and know each other's darkest secrets. There is a world of knowledge between them that I can't even attempt to understand. She's been with guys, before. Dated one pretty steadily for most of the time I shared their two bedroom apartment.

Luca didn't. He isn't with her—and doesn't seem like he wants to be—but he rarely sleeps with anyone without bringing Sun into it.

It works for them.

It doesn't work for me. Sharing isn't my thing. So I shut him down, and they became my best friends. My only friends, really. I don't have a lot of free time to socialize, and most people, when they find out who I work for, are too intent on that for me to get close to them.

"Where is English today?" Sun asks abruptly. Luca tenses on the other side of me.

"Audition. He was supposed to call me after. I'm starting to worry."

I can feel the look they exchange above my head, and I groan. "No you guys. It's not that."

"Sweetheart, it *should* be that," Sun says fervently.

I flick some beer at her and she smirks. "We don't want to see you hurt, Meg. You know it can happen. English isn't known for fidelity or longevity. And you're a country girl at heart," Luca says, pushing a lock of hair from my face.

"Which is why we have rules," I say, a little angry. "I'm not an idiot."

Luca laughs and shakes his head. His eyes are a little sad when he grabs my hand and pulls me from my stool. "Yes, you are, Megs. But you're our idiot, so try not to let him break your heart. I don't want to put you back together."

His hands are low on my hips, hugging me to him, and I can't feel Sun behind me—which means this is the most we've ever had, just the two of us. He rolls his hips into mine, in time with the music, a hand low on my back holding me to him. I shudder, and a dark smile touches his eyes.

I twist away, unwilling to face him, and he holds me close as we dance. His lips whisper the music in my ear, and for a while, the worry fades under the pressure of his hands and the soothing warmth of Sun's gaze.

Luca.

Sun is watching us, her dark eyes too knowing. I twist, turning Megan into the crowd as we dance. This is torture—there's nothing that can come of it, and getting myself turned on when I won't push her to act is a bad idea.

So why am I here, instead of with the blonde from the bar?

Megan's hips roll, and I groan, hardening against her. She laughs, a slow smoky noise, lifting an arm above her head to wrap around my neck.

What the hell? She tugs me down, closer to her, and I swallow hard and let go of all the reasons this is a bad idea. Push my dick against her ass. She shivers as I lean down, dropping a soft kiss on the nape of her neck. "What are you doing?" I ask, my voice low.

"Dancing." She giggles.

Ah. Those shots are working, then. "You don't dance like this, lovely girl," I murmur. "Not with me."

"Mmm." She nods and whimpers when I bite lightly on the curve of her neck. My hands skate up, thumbs brushing the curve of her breasts. "But I'm tired of watching you and Sun with strangers."

I don't respond, just hold her as we dance. It's nothing—not really. Her hands cover mine when they slip to rest low on her hips, and I can feel the tension that fills her.

My fingers are close, but not where she wants them. And she's just drunk enough to want them.

I'm not. And I won't cross that line with her until she's sober. I've waited too long for Megan to fuck it up over a few shots of tequila.

So I pet her, gently, until she's as turned on as I am. I tease and let her grind against my erection. And after a few songs, I catch Sun's eye and hand Megan over to her while I retreat to the bathroom and deal with the worst case of blue balls I've ever had.

Asher.

I delete the message.

Again.

It's asinine. I'm a top-tier actor. I could walk down any street, any day of the week, and have my pick of girls to shag. I could call any number of actresses and they'd be here in a few hours. So why, then, do I want the one woman who consistently ignores my flirting?

I'm a good flirt. I know I am. I know she notices.

What is especially asinine is that I am actually considering going out just to see her. Me. I *hate* going to clubs.

It's been over twenty-four hours since I saw her. My skin actually feels itchy and tight, my temper short. The ocean didn't even do its job of soothing me.

And I know what it is. I miss her.

I growl and head to the kitchen for a beer. My phone is still and black.

I'm a fucking idiot.

The doorbell rings, followed by an impatient rap that gets my hackles up. I want to turn away when a rough, masculine voice yells, "Open the damn door, English."

English.

I jerk it open, and a black man spills inside. A statuesque young woman in stilettos, black hair a sharp line around her face brightened by a streak of pink, and a silver scrap of material they're passing off as a dress stumbles in after him.

He's carrying Megan, her long hair spilling down his arm, one hand looped around his neck as she cuddles into him.

"Where the hell is the couch?" he mutters then makes a pleased noise and dumps her on my sofa.

Megan makes a sharp noise of surprise, and I shout, "Hey! What the bloody hell do you think you're doing?"

"Oh, god, Ash, keep your damn voice down," Meg whimpers.

The other girl giggles. "She said the tats weren't real."

I flush, looking down. I forgot I wasn't wearing a shirt.

"What the hell is going on?"

The man—the same one from the bar on New Year's Eve—points at her, "Megan insisted. She was too drunk to call—and I took her phone," he adds, completely unapologetic. I study him a little closer, and realization hits. I saw his head shot at the call back today.

"Luca James, right?"

He looks a little startled, but nods. "Yeah."

"I think we'll be working together."

Confusion clears. "On *Black Tides?* I heard they were talking to you."

I glance quickly at Megan—she looks like she's passed out.

Luca makes a slight disgruntled noise. "No, English. She doesn't talk about you or your work. I work in this town too. I hear things."

There's a crash from the kitchen, and Luca rolls his eyes. "Excuse me." He strides away. "Sun, get out of the man's fridge."

I turn back to the sofa and the girl snoring on it. What the hell is she doing here?

I crouch next to her and brush the hair from her face. "Drank too much," she mumbles.

"I see that." I laugh, softly. She nestles into my caress, and I go still, shocked. What. The. *Hell?*

"You didn't call. Was worried."

"It's your day off, Meggy. I didn't want to disturb you."

She giggles, a noise at odds with the no nonsense woman I'm used to seeing.

Of course, the girl in a slinky halter top, painted on jeans, and strappy heels, wasted on my couch, isn't what I'm used to seeing either.

"You're an idiot," she says clearly and then rolls over.

"Shit!" Luca curses. He shoves past me and grabs her around the waist, jerking her off the couch and into the kitchen. As I hear her throwing up, I decide I've fallen asleep and this is all a fucked up dream.

Chapter Four

Asher

She's still sleeping. I take a cup of hot tea and sit curled in a blanket on the back porch, inhaling the scent of the ocean and Earl Grey, and consider what to do. Megan will be furious when she wakes up and puts together the cluster fuck that was last night. I should feel bad—or, at least, attempt to get her and Luca and Sun off my sofa and into a cab home.

She's spent almost six months as my assistant, working with me and denying anything more than a working relationship, encouraging me to flirt with other girls and setting it up to have tabloids photograph us so the dates aren't wasted. She got my face out there—everyone knows who I am, and most don't even care that I'm a mite difficult to work with.

Megan did that.

But she ignored the attraction between us like her life depended on it. And after the last night, I am done with that shit.

I finish my tea, staring at the ocean and the waves, a small smile on my lips as I think about how far Louisiana is from Los Angeles, and how much I could do, trapped in a little car for days on end.

The door slides open behind me and I smile, twisting to look at her. And freeze.

Sun is gorgeous—all long legs, honey golden skin, and dark hair with that defiant streak of pink. A tattoo peeks out of the collar of her shirt, flirting with the curve of her neck. And she's wearing a t-shirt I dropped in the bathroom, the hem brushing the top of her thighs.

I swallow hard and look away, shoving my anger down. She's not who really angers me—it's girls like her. But this is Megan's friend, and that counts for something.

"You like the ocean?" she asks, sitting a few chairs over. I nod, staring out at it. "Megs grew up on the edge of a swamp—did she tell you that?"

I glance over at her, and Sun flashes a smile that sets my teeth on edge—knowing and a little devious, too *something* for me to be truly comfortable. "It's not that hard to miss you drooling over her, English."

There's that name again. "Why do you call me that?"

"When she started working for you, and we'd go out, she wanted a way to protect your identity while still talking about her life—and working with you *is* her life. So we took to calling you English. We knew who we were talking about but no one else did. It made her happy. Does it bother you?"

It doesn't, which is odd. Because Megan is the only one who has ever called me that, and usually when she's exhausted or furious or both—it's a slip, I realize.

"She's a lot more complex than I realized," I say. To myself.

Sun laughs softly. "She's a woman. Of course she is."

I glance at her, and this time, I don't see a pretty girl looking for sex—I see an anxious friend. "You're worried about her."

"Megan is a good girl—and she's a cutthroat bitch when she needs to be. But in a lot of ways, she's a sweetheart with a mile-wide streak of innocence. Don't fuck that up."

I blink. She stares at me for a few more minutes, her gaze hard and searching. Then she nods, almost to herself, and stands. "I'm gonna make a breakfast run. Want anything?"

The world to stop spinning in such confusing ways.

I shake my head, and she flashes a smile. I wonder, as she pads back inside, where she will find pants—and then I hear Megan's sleep-scratchy voice, and I don't fucking care.

Megan

Shit. Shit, fuck fuckity. What the hell had I been thinking, making Luca drive me *here* while I was drunk. Here of all fucking places. And now the bastard is playing least in sight, and my head hurts too damn much to do anything but make coffee and hope to hell he'll drive me home soon.

"You're up early." Sun murmurs, sliding the glass door shut behind her. "How you feeling, sweetheart?"

"Why on earth did we start doing shots? I'm too old for shots," I whine, leaning my head against the low hanging cabinet.

Sun chuckles, leaning down to kiss my cheek. "You say that every time we go out. I quit listening a long time ago."

I want to glare at her, but it would mean moving, and I'm not doing that until my coffee is finished.

"Hey. No kissing unless I get to watch," Luca says. I feel him enter the room, and the look he gives Sun. I grab my mug of coffee as the Kuerig finishes and scoot to one side to doctor it.

Asher keeps my creamer—all three—on hand. He learned quickly I'm not pleasant when deprived of coffee.

"I'll be back. Going to forage," Sun chirps. I hear the clink of keys and then she's gone.

And the tension in the room climbs. I shift farther away, and Luca sighs. "Why are you running, Megs?"

"I'm not."

A lie. A big, fat one that we're both going to ignore because I'm a coward and he's a good friend. And he had me riding the edge of orgasm on the dance floor last night.

I glance out to the back porch. Knox is sitting there, hair hanging in his face, looking lost.

All the worry I felt last night, the thing that drove me here, comes bubbling back, and I take a step toward the door before I realize I've moved.

"You can't run from both of us," Luca murmurs softly. Low enough I can pretend I didn't hear it as he brushes a kiss over the top of my head and steps away. "I'm going to shower."

I nod absently and watch Asher, his fingers drumming on the wooden chair.

I sip my coffee and gather the scraps of my dignity like a shield. Taking a deep breath, I head outside.

Knox looks up as I sit down next to him, staring at me with unabashed frankness. I blow on my coffee and murmur, "Stop, creeper."

"Says the girl who showed up on my doorstep drunk at two am."

I hear the smile in his voice and finally look up.

"You aren't mad?"

Surprise flickers across his face. "Why would I be?"

"I showed up unannounced in the middle of the night. Most of our clients would be pissed—especially since I came with two friends."

A smile plays across his lips. "Is that what you're worried about? Meggy, I don't care how or when you come to me—as long as you do."

I feel heat creep up my cheeks, and I look away from him, at the ocean beginning to brighten with the day and the joggers pounding down the sand. "Why do you say things like that?" I ask then bite my tongue. Stupid question. I must still be hungover.

I hear his intake of breath. It takes everything to not look at him, because I've seen him like this—the naked hunger in his eyes, the emotions so open it hurts. I love that look on him.

People think they see him—the real him with his half smiles and bashful boy grins. With his eyes blazing with lust and anger.

But they don't. If they saw him, right now. They'd know.

Except, it's a lie. This is just another act for him—he plays a part because that's what Knox does. What he's so damn good at.

"Never mind," I say crisply. "What happened at the call back?"

"They gave me the lead," he says, tuneless.

I want to cheer. Maybe that will make Kevin happy for a few days. "And you took it?"

He nods. "Megan?"

I glance at him, questioning.

"You promised."

I swallow hard, and he leans into me, taking the coffee from my limp fingers and pressing a kiss to my cheek. I tremble at the sudden invasion of my space, the flouting of the rules I've carefully established. His breath is warm against my ear, and I want to bask in it for days. "It's because you blush—the prettiest pink I've ever seen. I'd do just about anything to see that."

His lips press, chaste and somehow erotic, against my skin, and then he pulls away, a smile dancing in his eyes as he stands and leaves the porch. I lean slowly back in my chair and close my eyes, trying not to feel that kiss.

I should be terrified about spending a week with him in a car.

And, distantly, I am.

But I'm also just turned on enough to wonder what the hell could happen between here and Branton.

Sweet Ruin

Chapter Five

Asher

I slouch in the chair in Kevin's ornate office, a pair of aviators low on my nose. The contract's have been signed—I've given Lion House three months of my life, if filming stays on schedule—and Kevin is all but rubbing his hands together in glee.

Good. Because he's going to hate this.

"Megan and I will need my limo for the next week and a half."

Kevin pauses in the middle of pouring a glass of champagne. The good shit, too—Dom. He can afford it.

"I don't think heading cross country with your assistant is the best idea you've ever had, Ash."

"She promised," I say, and it sounds petulant.

"She had no authority to promise that. She's not even a junior agent—she's a coffee girl."

I bristle. It's one thing to talk to me like I'm an idiot. I don't like it, but what the fuck ever. It's another thing entirely to talk about Megan. "She's the best PA I've ever had and does above and beyond her job—I've gotten more press since she started than in the year before that."

Anger colors Kevin's cheeks. He doesn't like when I sing the praises of his niece. "Disappearing for a month isn't a good way to keep that going."

He doesn't get it. I frown, annoyed, as I sit up. "Kevin, I'm not asking. I'm telling you—you work for me, remember. And I'm leaving for a few weeks. I'll be in New Orleans for the start of filming. That's all that matters."

"Fine," he grits out, setting the champagne down in front of me. I take it warily, waiting for the other shoe to drop. He isn't giving up—Kevin Hart doesn't know how. But he doesn't say anything else, and I don't think he intends to. After a long minute, I flash a smile and pick up my champagne. He clinks our glasses lightly, and I lift it to my lips, inhaling fizz and the bitter beverage.

"Megan isn't going with you. I'm transferring her off your account," Kevin says casually, and I go still. I swallow the champagne that tastes like ashes and force myself to shrug. To not react—he doesn't get to see my panic and rage.

"Fine. Send my new PA to New Orleans in a few weeks." I put the glass down and stretch to my full height, buttoning my suit coat as I flash him a final cool smile, and stalk from the office.

I'm almost out the front doors when I hear my name being called. I take two more steps, and a hand grabs my arm. I glance over my shoulder, expecting to find Kevin standing there with a disgruntled expression.

Luca James.

What the fuck. Why does he keep turning up, and can I get rid of him?

"What's wrong?" Luca says immediately, pushing the door open and waiting as I step outside.

"What makes you think anything is?" I snap.

"It took me calling your name four times to get your attention, and you look pissed." Luca arches an eyebrow. "And you came from Kevin's office. Something has to be wrong."

"He's taking Meggy away," I say, and saying it out loud makes it real in a way it hadn't been. My stomach dips and, for a second, I think I'll throw up, the nausea is so strong.

I can't do this without her—I don't even want to. The shine of the bright lights wore off a long time ago. Now they just hurt my eyes.

"What the hell are you talking about?" Luca hisses.

Briefly, I fill him in on the conversation with Kevin and the promise Megan made. I shake my head, not quite believing the words I'm saying. I can't tell her this.

I don't realize I've said that out loud until Luca shrugs and smirks. "So don't tell her."

I glance back at him. He has an odd expression—his smile somewhere between savage and insane. "What are you talking about?"

"She won't go, if you tell her. And this trip is as good for her as it is for you. Would you really take that from her?"

"So you want me to lie?"

"Not lie so much as, don't mention it. Kevin won't, not until you're on the road—it'd mean dealing with Megs and hiring someone new, and he's not that invested in replacing her. He's bluffing and trying to get you to back down, while reminding both of you that he has you by the balls. Might be good to remind him the same is equally true."

I stare at Luca, open mouthed. He smirks and slides a business card into my front pocket. "Take her to this resort. She'll love it. And then bring her to Vegas—I'll calm her down, and you can go on your merry way."

I almost ask him why he's bothering to help me—what's in it for him? But I don't. I don't want to know.

Luca

"What do you mean, you're leaving?"

I glance at Sun. "I mean Ash and Megan are about to head cross country for a month. I'm going with them."

Sun frowns. "Meg didn't mention anything like that."

I stop in the middle of packing and stare at her. "I haven't told her. But she promised Ash this trip, and Kevin is threatening to pull her from his account and—"

"And you saw an opportunity to make your move."

I hesitate.

"Are you going to tell her the truth?" she asks, applying another layer of polish to her toe.

I don't respond. I've spent a lot time—eighteen months, to be precise—avoiding telling Megan the truth. I've let her think I'm in love with Sun, that I'm a player and content with the friend zone I've been relegated to.

"Sun, are you going to tell her?"

"That you're manipulating her?" she asks, looking up. I swallow hard, because whatever my reasons, that's what it comes down to.

"No."

My breath rushes from me, and I feel dizzy, suddenly. "Why not?"

She flashes me a tiny smile. "Because she makes you happy—happy in a way you haven't been since Dylan."

I flinch, and she rises, walking on her heels to stand at my side. "I want you to be happy, Luca. Even if it's not with me." She kisses my cheek and walks away, throwing over her shoulder, "But if you hurt her, I'll break your legs."

I grin—she would.

Megan

I park in the driveway and stalk to the front door, pounding on it briefly before peeking inside. The foyer is, predictably, empty. I tap my nails then climb the stairs. "Knox, what's the emergency?" I ask.

"I'm in my closet."

That stirs my interest, and I make my way to his huge walk-in closet. He's standing in the middle of it, wearing a gray suit and pale green linen shirt. He's knotting a slim gray tie, brows drawn in concentration.

"What are you doing?" I ask, grinning at him.

"You up for a short trip?" he asks. I arch an eyebrow, silently questioning, and he laughs. "I have a photo shoot in San Diego. You should come with me."

I frown. "I don't remember Kevin telling me about that."

"It just sprang up."

"Ok. When are we leaving?"

He smoothes down his tie and smiles at me. "Right now."

I blink, startled, and then shrug. Part of being the bottom of the totem pole is having to deal with shit as it comes up—and it's not like I had a crazy busy weekend planned. "Can we go by my house to get some stuff?"

He hesitates, and I go still, watching him. Finally, Knox nods and smiles. "Of course."

I take a step toward the door, and he crowds into me, his breath warm on my neck. "Do you still want to get out of town?" he asks.

I lick suddenly dry lips and nod. "Yes. I know you still need to, which is the most important thing."

Something flickers in his eyes briefly, and he nods, stepping back and grabbing his overnight bag. "Let's go."

He follows me across town to my little bungalow. For a brief moment, I have a flash of insecurity over my tiny two bedroom rental, on a rundown street without a spectacular view. If Ash has any thoughts about it, he doesn't comment. He stands quiet next to me, head low as I unlock the door and usher him into the cool, dark interior.

It's messy, dishes in the sink from when Sun cooked a few nights ago. "Sorry," I mutter.

Asher cuts a look in my direction, then pursues the place. His gaze takes it all in—the table covered in newspapers and magazines, the blanket on the couch, and my heels kicked off by the door. The lazily spinning fan and candles with wicks that badly need trimming.

"I love it," he says, his voice husky. I blink, a little startled. He gives me a lopsided smile and nods at the back hall. "Get ready. I'll wait here."

I nod, trying to get a good grasp on his emotions and mood, but he's a remote and closed off. It makes me nervous, but I don't push him.

In my bedroom, I grab my phone and type quickly.

Me: English wants me to keep him company on a weekend trip. And then I'm headed home for a few weeks. Want to do lunch Monday before I head out of town?

I shoves some clothes, cute underwear, and a clean set of PJs into a bag and head to the bathroom. My travel bag is already packed, so I snag it and some makeup off the counter before dumping it into my small suitcase. A few pairs of shoes go in, and then my phone vibrates.

Sun: I can. Luca has a gig in Vegas, so he'll be out of town.

Me: Ok. I'll call you on Monday.

Sun: Do you want me to check on the house while you're gone?

I smile—this is what I love about Sun. One of the many things.

Me: Please.

That done, I tuck my phone back into my pocket and grab a couple sweater dresses and tights. That'll have to be enough.

Once I've added chargers and my computer to my messenger bag, I heft the tote and head back to the living room.

Asher is standing at my sink, wearing a ridiculous apron as he scrubs my pots and stacks dishes in the washer.

I set the bag down and stare at him. "What are you doing?"

"Mum always hated to come home to a mess," he says, "and since it's my fault you're leaving so quickly—I thought I could help sort it out first."

He's right. I do hate coming home to a mess. But. "Knox, you don't have to do that," I protest quietly.

Ash glances over his shoulder and gives me a close lipped smile. "I want to."

Not much to say to that. I lean against the counter and watch silently as he finishes cleaning my kitchen, wiping the counters and emptying the sink trap before washing and drying his hands. Then he turns and gives me a pleased smile. "Ready?"

I wonder, briefly, if I really am.

But it's too late now to back out.

Asher

She's nervous—I can feel the edginess coming off her in waves. She shifts in her seat, her phone clutched anxiously in her hand. We've barely even left the apartment, and already she wants to bolt.

My phone buzzes.

Luca: Did you leave?

I smirk. The black man is almost as invested in this as I am.

Me: Yes.

Luca: Don't tell her anything until you get to the resort. She'll worry herself to sleep soon. Keep her safe, English.

I roll my eyes and drop my phone back into my lap.

"Who was that?" she asks, her voice startling me out of my thoughts. I slide a glance over and see her staring at me with those gorgeous green eyes. She's worried, her lip caught between her teeth.

"A friend," I say and click on the radio. I see the surprise in her eyes, and I feel a pang—I'm being rude. I want to explain what I'm doing—I want to explain everything. But I can't. Not yet.

So I let the music wash through the car and drive into the waning day. And if I breathe a little easier when I see her relax and slump, her soft, steady breaths filling the little sports car, it's only because I feel like I'm lying—and I hate that.

Its pitch black outside when I finally stop. Megan blinks slowly, and I go still, watching her. She looks confused, staring out at the dark villa.

"Where are we?" she asks.

I take a deep breath, let it out slowly. "A villa. Just north of the border—I booked it for the next two days."

For a moment, it's like she hasn't heard me. Then she jerks upright, her cheeks flushed an angry red, and her words come out like ice. "What the *fuck*, Knox?"

Oh. There's that again. "Go inside and get settled," I say quietly, not looking at her. "I'll explain everything in the morning."

"What about your photo shoot?" she snaps.

I glance at her, and she laughs, a disbelieving little noise. "You bastard," she says, softly. Then she steps out of the car, slamming the door hard enough to shake the frame. I wince. I don't care about the car—it's the least of my concerns, frankly. But I do worry about her and how angry she must be.

I pick up my phone and dial.

"Are you there?" Luca says. His voice is thick and gravelly, almost as if I woke him. Of course, it's almost midnight—maybe I did wake him.

"Yes. She pissed, man. Are you sure this is a good idea?"

I had wanted to bolt for Branton and the anonymity of her hometown. It was Luca's idea to reroute to a villa for a few days. Kevin wouldn't look to the south for her—and when he realized I'd gone off without waiting for his arrangements, he *would* look for me. Kevin didn't do well without constant supervision.

"She'll come around," Luca says, his voice confident. "And when you leave there you're meeting me in Vegas. I'll keep her from bolting once you get her back to civilization."

"What makes you think she won't before then?"

"You're remote. And you have a manicurist coming to see her tomorrow—she won't go anywhere."

It annoys me somewhat that he knows that—he knows her well enough to call her moods. I want to know her that well.

"English—this is important. You aren't there to seduce her."

What? Cock blocked from fucking Vegas? "Who said anything about seducing her?" He laughs, the bastard. I can't help smirking. "Dude. Gorgeous villa on the ocean. What else is there to do?"

"I will personally kick your ass," Luca says crisply, without heat. "Keep your hands off her until you get to Vegas."

"Wanna watch?" I taunt him, and he laughs, a low noise that shouldn't be a turn on.

Luca

"Would you let me?" I ask, my voice dropping to a murmur. There's a telling silence from the other end of the phone, and I have an *oh shit* moment. Then my phone beeps.

There she is. Right on cue.

"I gotta run, English," I say, forcing my tone to go normal. Let him think I'm fucking around. Works for me, as long as he brings her where I want.

He says something, but I'm already clicking over and it's lost.

"Hey, Megs. What's going on?"

"Are you awake? I just—I need help."

Even knowing what's going on, every nerve in my body tenses at the desperation in her voice.

"What's wrong?"

"I'm at a villa north of the border. The English bastard decided he wanted a weekend away." She sounds so disgusted and disgruntled, and I can hear bottles clinking together.

"What are you talking about?"

"Asher Fucking Knox. Told me he had a photo shoot and drove me to the middle of fucking nowhere, and now I'm trapped." Her pitch goes up a little, furious and a little scared. "Come get me."

I make a sympathetic noise. "Lovely girl, I can't. I'm on a gig, remember?"

"Shit." she mutters. "And Sun…"

"With Pablo for the weekend," I fill in. The clinking pauses, and I grin. "Are you stealing from his mini-bar?"

"He stole me," she mutters, and I do laugh. "Quit it, Luca." I sober and hear her sigh. "What do I do?"

My nerves string tight. She sounds lost and on the verge of tears. I'm no good with that—and I want to save her. That's my job—has been since I saw her in her uncle's office eighteen months ago, furious and frightened.

"Megs. Give the guy a chance. He's not going to rape and kill you—and you just told me the other day that you were planning on going back to Branton with him, right? How is this different?"

"I didn't do this!" she almost yells. "It was completely out of my hands, and he lied to get me here."

I take a deep breath, trying to calm down. Getting as angry as she is won't help anyone—especially not her. "Try to see the upside of this, Megs."

"What upside?"

"Oh, I don't know. You're with one of the most attractive men in Hollywood, at a deserted beach. I could find a few upsides."

"It's not like that between us. You know it's not."

I lose an aggravated sigh. "It's not because you won't let it be. Asher wants you. You're scared to let him—or anyone else—get close to you."

I hear her sharp intake of breath, can easily picture her wide, hurt eyes. I sigh.

"I have those rules for a reason," she says, her voice surprisingly steady. "Kevin doesn't take me serious. If I sleep with my clients—"

"What about me?" I ask, before I can stop myself. Then the question is out there and I can't take it back, so I run with it. "What about the way you shut down before even giving us a chance."

She's quiet, and I curse. "Just, for once, take a chance."

"That isn't fair," she whispers.

"And what you did, shoving me away because of Sun—that was? That's bullshit, and we both know it."

"Why are you doing this?" she demands.

Why? Why now? When Kevin is minutes from firing her, and I have nothing left to lose? "Because if I lose you, I at least want to know I tried. I fought for you first."

She makes a choked little noise, and I know it's enough—too much, probably. I've pushed too hard.

"Just promise you'll have fun. Don't sleep with him if you don't want to, but relax. Enjoy it. You deserve to relax and have fun every once in a while."

She makes a soft noise that could be an assent—or maybe she's telling me to go fuck myself. Either way, I need to let her go.

"I'll call you tomorrow, after the shoot. Okay?"

"'kay."

I want to reassure her, but I don't. I make myself hang up and release a sigh, slowly. I stand and pad to the window, staring out at Vegas and wishing like hell I was on a beach in south Cali with Megan.

Sweet Ruin

Chapter Six

Megan

I manage, against my good sense and own desire, to fall asleep. It's after only three mini bottles of vodka and one bottle of cranberry juice. So I'm blissfully un-hungover the next morning.

With the sun shining too bright in my eyes, I jerk a pillow over my face and groan. I don't want to deal with the morning—or Asher. Or what Luca said last night, which I'd like to ignore. It keeps playing on a loop in my head, his voice soft and warm and painfully demanding.

I don't want to think he's telling the truth.

But when was the last time I was in a relationship more satisfying than the one I have with my vibrator? I had dated a guy, semi-seriously, in college, but he'd been happy in Branton, and I wanted—needed—more. I still do. And while there were a few guys who caught my eye, and even some I took to bed, they were temporary distractions that quickly got replaced by my work.

Luca and Sun were the only constants in my life since coming to LA. And work, but that doesn't count, especially since I refused to entertain thoughts of relationships with clients.

I sigh and thumb through my messages and notifications. There are a few from Kevin, all with the same basic message—call him.

I roll out of bed and head to my bathroom. I didn't investigate last night, but a quick look shows a spacious bathroom with a Jacuzzi tub big enough for five people. Without thinking, I snap a picture and send a text.

Me: You would have so much fun with this place.

Then I strip out of my wrinkled t-shirt and jeans and step into the hot shower.

The water is soothing, just a degree short of too hot, and as it pounds against my skin, I let myself think about what Luca said and making the best of it. I stare critically at my nails and assess my wet hair. "Fuck it," I mutter. "If I have to be here, might as well enjoy it."

And since sunbathing in January isn't my cup of tea—even in south Cali—a massage and mani/pedi seems like just the ticket. Asher won't want to do that. So I can pamper myself and relax *and* avoid the root of all evil.

This epic fail might just turn into a win. With a smug smile, I finish rinsing shampoo from my hair and step out of the shower. I glance at my phone—another text came in from Kevin, and one from Luca.

> **Luca:** Only if you in it. ;)
> **Me:** Perv
> **Luca:** You like me that way.

I breathe a laugh and shimmy into my underwear and bra. A cute pair of jeans and off the shoulder sweater finish my ensemble. My phone buzzes, and I glance at it.

Yeah. It's not a good idea to talk to my uncle without at least half a cup of coffee. I tuck it back into my butt pocket and venture out of my room.

I can smell the scent of the ocean—Asher has the back door propped open. The boy doesn't seem to know how to close a door. There's a tray of covered dishes on the counter, and I step toward it, drawn by the scent of food and rich coffee. I peek under a few and find waffles, fresh fruit, fluffy eggs and hash browns, biscuits, sausage, bacon and ham. A small bowl of yogurt and another of grits that makes my mouth water. It's like he picked everything off the room service menu.

"I didn't know what you wanted."

I glance over my shoulder and eye him. He's wearing sleep pants, hanging low on his hips, and a thin white t-shirt. His hair is mussed, a little bit of scruff on his defined jaw. Tattoos snake down his arms, are faintly visible through his shirt.

He looks for all the world like a fallen angel, and it strikes me that I am maybe the only girl in the world who wouldn't let him seduce her.

I grit my teeth and look back at the food. "Have you eaten?"

"No. I was waiting on you."

I bite back a sigh and turn away. He's moved, and frames me with his body, blocking me in. "Don't be mad, Meggy. Please."

"You lied to me, Knox. How on earth do you think I won't be mad?"

"I do have a photo shoot. I rescheduled it for here."

I stare at him, deadpan, and he has the grace to flush. "You work too hard. You worked through the holidays—even New Years. You deserve to relax. And you can do that here."

I shove him lightly, uncomfortable with his nearness. "I could do that in my house with a tub of Ben and Jerry's and Netflix. Sun and I need to catch up on *Breaking Bad.*"

I grab two plates, and Asher catches me around the waist, drawing me back against him. I go stiff, fury coursing in my veins. What the fuck? "You don't get to touch me. You don't get to grab me and take me from my life and then try to break the rules. It doesn't work that way."

"I wanted to give you something."

I jerk out of his arms and take a few steps away, giving myself room to breathe. He keeps talking, his tone urgent. "You've done so much, Megs. And this role for *Black Tides*—it's a game changer. We both know that."

It is.

"Then send me a box of Godiva, for crying out loud. Don't abduct me and take me to a fucking resort."

He winces and rubs a hand over his hair. "I'm sorry. You're right—I fucked up."

I snort and sit down at the bar, sliding a fork toward him. "Don't worry. I'm visiting a spa—this place does have a spa, right?—and putting it on the room."

A smile spreads across his face, and he lowers himself into the chair next to me as I begin uncovering dishes.

Oh god. I'm gonna need to exercise for a week, after this meal. I shove that thought aside and dig into the waffles. Screw it. Right now, I'm on a forced vacation with one of the hottest guys I've ever met, and I refuse to think about anything but enjoying myself. At a hefty price tag, that I send straight to Asher.

My phone buzzes again, and I sigh, grabbing it. I'm startled to see Atticus's name blinking at me instead of Kevin, and I answer quickly.

"Hi!"

"Hey, sweetheart. How are you?"

Atti sounds like he always does—a little distracted and happy to hear from me. And sexy as sin.

I'm not supposed to think that about my sister's ex-husband, or my previous professor. But with Atti, it's hard not to at least *notice*.

"You got my message?"

"Yeah. Of course, whenever you're in town, just give me a call. I'd love to see you—and your client. Who does Kevin have you working with? Anyone I know?"

I glance at Knox, who's watching me with wide eyes. "Just an English actor new to the agency. But you'll talk to him?"

"For you? Anything. I've wanted to call, but…"

"But in a divorce, Nik gets to keep her family. I know. She'll be pissed when she finds out I called you—so remind her that I think you're awful and should rot in hell."

He laughs. "Don't I? I left her, not the other way around."

"No, Atti," I say, my voice warming slightly. "I love her, but I'm not under any illusions ok? What Nik did was ten different kinds of fucked up—you were completely within your rights."

There's a moment of quiet and then, "I'm with someone, now."

That's a surprise. Because it's been less than a year since their marriage imploded, and only three months since the divorce was finalized. "That's…fast."

"She's important to me."

I take a moment to process that. "Is she good to you?"

"Yes."

"Then that's all that matters." I remember someone and grin. "Does Dane like her?"

Atti groans. "When they aren't at each other's throats, he loves her."

I laugh, and he makes a disgruntled sound. "I'll call you when we get to town, then."

After I hang up, Asher cocks his head at me. "He sounds like more than a professor, Meggy."

I pick at the fruit on our plate—he's eaten all the apples and grapes. Good riddance. "Atticus married my sister when I was in high school. We were close—I was friends with his sister. They've been part of my life for a long time."

"And?"

"And he's like a brother—I don't have one, and he became that."

He watches me closely. "You love him."

"But I'm not in love with him. Huge difference, Knox."

Some of the tension slides out of him, and he glances down at my phone as it rings. Again.

Asher

Kevin. *Fuck.* I didn't think it would be this fast.

"Shit. He's been trying to get ahold of me all morning." She reaches for the phone. I swipe it from her.

"Kevin. What can I do for you?" I say, standing and walking away from Megan. She's quiet, watching me.

There's a beat of silence, and then, "I told you I was taking her off your account. What the hell are you doing? Where is she?"

"She doesn't know that. It might have been a stupid move, telling me first. And before you tell me about the grand scheme you have, I'm not interested."

"You can't decide that."

I scoff. "I'm Asher fucking Knox, Kevin. I can decide whatever the hell I want."

Annoyed, I hit the end button and turn back to Megan.

"What aren't you telling me?" she asks, her eyes narrowed.

So much. I swallow hard.

"You don't want to know yet, Meggy. And I promise, after your spa day—I'll tell you everything."

She pales and swallows hard. "Did he fire me?"

"*No*. And if he wants to keep me as a client, he won't. But he is unhappy—and that is on me. Just give me today. Please?"

She bites her lip, and I want to kiss it. I want to drag her into my room and kiss her until she can't remember all the reasons we won't work. Instead, I clench my hands into tight fists and wait for her to make up her mind.

Finally she sighs and glances down at her toes. "Fine. But only 'cause I really want my toes to look pretty again."

I grin through a rush of relief. She stands and walks past me to her room. I catch the scent of her hair, warm and clean, and I suppress a shiver. She hesitates then goes up on tip toes, her lips brushing against my cheek, a ghost-light touch. I do shiver then, and she smirks as she drops back down on her feet. "Thanks for breakfast," she says over her shoulder, and I mumble something—even I don't understand what. Her laugh is a soft noise that chases me across the kitchen and into my own room. There I sit on the bed and try to get a grip on my erection and emotions.

It was barely a kiss—I've had more action on a screen test. So why can this girl get such a reaction from me? Why is Megan so fucking different?

I dial the front desk. "I need an appointment for the day."

When Megan comes back out of her room, I'm sitting on the couch, my tablet in my lap while I read the script, highlighting important scenes. "You aren't supposed to be working this weekend," she says dryly.

"Does that mean you stayed off the blogs and didn't answer email?" I ask, darting a look up at her. She makes a face, and I laugh. "I need something to do while you're getting pampered, darling."

"Read a book," she deadpans.

I drop the script and lean forward. "I'll come with you."

She snorts. I stare at her until she finally looks away. "You're insane, you know that, Knox?" she murmurs. It's a rhetorical question. But I nod. "I have rules, you know. Those haven't gone away just because we did."

"I am well aware of you rules."

"Are you? Because you didn't seem to care earlier."

I smile at her, a slow, easy smile. "You forget, Meggy. Those are your rules. I've respected them because I respect you. But I know what I want, and I'm tired of waiting for you to wake up. I won't push you further than you want me to—but I'm done ignoring what we have."

Her mouth has fallen open, and she's staring at me like she hasn't seen me before. I give her a quick smile and sit back. "So what's it going to be, Meggy? Am I working today, or am I spending it with you?"

Chapter Seven

Luca

"Okay, that's it"

I smirk as the blonde model in skinny jeans and pasties peels herself—slowly—off my chest. She's all blonde hair, creamy skin, and come-hither eyes. I step away from her, my smile slipping from the one I use for cameras to the cool professionalism that keeps girls like her from thinking I want more when the cameras quit.

I don't. A quick fuck with a pretty girl isn't worth the drama, and I get tired of Megan's sad smile when I get caught with my pants down.

I check my phone for what seems like the millionth time today, a little pissed off there isn't a waiting message. I shouldn't be mad—the resort was my idea, after all—but it rankles, to know I've been replaced so quickly and easily.

"Want to get a drink?" Aria asks, pulling a plain white tank top on. Even in that, barefoot and her hair disheveled, she's slinging sex appeal like second nature.

"Can't. I've got another gig tomorrow."

"You sure that's it? I heard from one of the other girls you have commitment problems."

I give her a flat smile and walk away. Call it what you want, I wasn't going near the girl with a ten-foot pole, not once the cameras went down.

Not for the first time, I wish I'd invited Sun. Then I remember why I didn't, and I close my eyes. I don't want to think about her. I don't want to think at all.

In my room, I flop onto the bed and stare at the ceiling and wonder what the hell she's doing.

Megan

We spend the day in the spa. Asher reads a magazine and makes a few comments about the color choice of my toe nails, but for the most part, he just watches. It's distracting at first, but then I say *fuck it* and give myself over to the pure relaxation of being pampered. I tune out the English man as I drift in bliss.

"You want a trim and color?" an attendant asks, peeking into the room.

I nod and hear the chair where Ash is sitting creak. "I like your hair color."

"I want highlights." I say. For the first time. I consider that this is costing a small fortune, and then I remember that he lied to get me here. I lift my head up as the massage therapist works my shoulders. I'm mostly naked. and I clutch the sheet shielding me. "You don't get to vote, remember?"

"I voted on your toes," he protests.

Men are idiots. "Toes are easy to change, Ash." I let my head drop down, groaning as the masseuse works out a particularly deep knot.

Asher mutters something indistinct, and I smirk to myself.

"Fine. I'll move our dinner reservations."

I glance at him. "I don't want to go to dinner," I say.

Asher smirks. "I'm not asking for much, Meggy. But I do want the ability to show you off tonight. You won't really deny me that, will you?"

"I'm not yours to show off, Knox," I say, letting my head drop lazily.

He laughs, sitting back. "You remind me of that as often as you can. But they have fresh oysters and steak."

My stomach growls, a reminder that I ate breakfast, but not nearly enough before I bolted from table in a fit of anger and disgust.

"Maybe I wanted to spend some alone time with you," I say, and Asher laughs, a husky noise that stirs my languid blood.

"Darling, if that's what you want, you just need to say so. But it's not, and we both know it."

I shrug, and the masseuse smacks my shoulder. I yelp. Asher gives me a dry smile.

"Fine," I say, settling back on the table. "Change our reservations."

He leaves while I'm getting my hair cut, and for the first time, I can inhale without worry or concern. I glance at my phone as the hairdresser shifts around me, trimming and sniping away dead ends. I'm not making a drastic change—I'm not the kind of girl to walk in and cut six inches off at one time.

"Your boyfriend is very attentive, isn't he?" the stylist says.

I laugh, softly. "He isn't my boyfriend."

"Most who come here are on their honeymoon."

"We aren't most," I say cryptically. The stylist gives me a polite smile, and it could mean anything—that I'm an idiot for walking away from such a handsome man who so clearly wants me, or maybe it's as simple as she doesn't believe me.

I probably wouldn't, if I were her.

As I sit, waiting for my highlights to set, I text Sun.

Me: Have you talked to Luca?

Sun: Not today? Have you? He's being crazy, Meggy.

I frown. What the hell? It's been less than a week since we went out together—how much could change in just a few days?

Me: What's going on?

Sun: He moved out. Didn't he tell you?

I stare in shock. How had I talked to him last night without him even hinting at that? How had I not noticed something amiss with him? And why the fuck would he do that? Sun was his center, the thing that kept him grounded and focused when shit got crazy—and in Hollywood, as a working actor, shit got crazy all the fucking time.

Me: Are you sure it's permanent? He's not just…I don't know, experimenting again? Remember, he did that when I first moved in.

Sun: He took everything. He says he's going back to St. Paul after _Black Tides._

Well, fuck.

"Ok, let's rinse you," my stylist says brightly, and I type a quick response.

Me: Gotta run—I'll call him.

Then I pocket my phone and try to shut off my mind for a little longer.

Luca isn't answering his phone when I call. I try four times in the time it takes me to walk from the spa to our villa. And Asher's pulled a vanishing act. Annoyed, feeling tension pulling in my shoulders, I stalk to my room and come to an abrupt halt.

The dress is soft and flirty, a silk backless halter top and flowing skirt that rests at mid-thigh, all in a blue so deep it could only be called midnight.

A heavy shawl rests folded next to it.

The heels are a vibrant red—fuck me heels.

Asher Knox is playing dress up. A smile curves my lips. Well, at least the boy has good taste.

I shimmy out of my jeans and top and step into the dress. It fits like a glove, and I'm briefly annoyed that Ash has noticed my measurements. I'm not focusing—my thoughts are pin-balling all over the place, and that's a bad place to be when I'm sitting down with Knox for an evening. I can't afford distraction.

Not even the current cluster-fuck that is my best friends and their relationship.

I sit on the bed and take a deep breath, focusing.

He's a client. An attractive, moody client. Kevin will never take me serious if I sleep with the talent—no one will. I'll always be the girl who fucked her way to the top.

I refuse to be that girl. I came here to get away from one image people have of me—I get to decide the next one. I won't use sex as a weapon or a tool—I will not become my sister.

There's a tap on my door. "I'll be right there, Knox."

He doesn't say anything, just retreats.

No touching. No relationships. No contact when I'm not working. This whole weekend is breaking every rule I have. With a sigh, I stand and open the door.

Asher stops, turning to face me. His eyes go wide when he sees me, and I wonder if I'm disappointing. He offers me a lopsided smile. "You look gorgeous, Meggy."

I flush and look down. "You aren't supposed to notice that," I scold. "You're Asher Knox, for crying out loud. Have a little decorum."

"What's the good of being a movie star if you don't get to use the lines on the pretty girls?"

I give him a dry look. "Your scripts have better lines than that."

He laughs, coming around me to place the shawl on my shoulders. I shiver as his hands linger, a little too tight and too long. "But none have quite as much honesty—and you like honesty, pet."

I don't respond, because he's right. And because I'm fighting back the feel of his touch.

"Phone?"

My gaze comes up, startled, and he grins. "We're gonna try something new. No phones for the next two hours. I get you without distractions or defenses—and your phone is the biggest distraction and defense you have. So hand it over."

"Knox," I say slowly.

"Kevin hasn't called you since this morning, right? The world won't end if you put the electronics down for two hours, Meggy."

It might—mine, anyway. But his gaze is pleading, and I find myself fishing the little device out of my bra and handing it over. His fingers caress the warm plastic case, and I know what he's thinking—the same thing I'm thinking—*that was just in my bra.* His eyes darken a little, but he doesn't say anything as he tucks it into a drawer and opens the front door. "Ready?"

I nod, and he leads me out of the villa and down the private beach. We walk side by side, arms brushing, silent as he leads us to a small building. It's eerily quiet, and I hesitate on the sand, staring at it.

"Is it closed?"

He shakes his head. "I bought out the night."

My eyebrows shoot up. "What happened to wanting to show me off?"

He shrugs. "You aren't mine to show off—and when I started thinking about it, I decided I didn't want to share you. I didn't want to worry about people taking our pictures and interrupting, thinking they have the right to. I just want to have dinner with you. Is that ok?"

I stare at him, searching his face for the lie—for the hint that this is just another part of the game he's playing to get me into bed, but it's heartbreakingly open. And I see nothing there but a plea for understanding.

There's a question, lingering on the tip of my tongue, and I want to ask him. But I follow him inside the dark restaurant and let the hostess seat us in the corner booth. Soft jazz is playing, low candles burn on each table, and a low light hangs in a wire light fixture, pieces of crystal catching and throwing the light beams dizzily, and I wonder how much it cost. Asher snaps his fingers lightly in front of my face, and I jerk, looking at him.

"You have a question."

I frown, and he smirks. "You aren't the only one who notices things, Meggy."

Fair enough.

"Why are you doing this? Is it simply to get in my pants? I promise it's not worth all of this," I say, gesturing at the empty room.

He laughs, and I sit back. A waitress approaches and sets a bottle of sangria on the table for us. I pour a glass, and lift it to my lips, watching as the amusement fades in Knox's eyes.

"Why do you think that's the only reason?"

"Because you're a twenty four year old guy?"

"Fair point. But it's not why--you know I want you, Megan. I haven't tried to hide that. I've respected your rules. But I haven't lied. And I've gotten to know you, as much as you'll let me."

"And what do you think you know about me."

He hesitates, and cocks his head. "No. I'm not playing this game, unless there are some real stakes to it."

My pulse spikes, and I lick my lips. "Like what?"

"If I am right, I get a kiss."

I feel, suddenly, like I'm at a frat party again, playing strip poker and other drinking games. "And if you're wrong?"

"I'll do a shot."

He can't know that much about me. It's not like I tell him everything—how bad can this possibly be?

"Fine," I say, and signal to the waitress. "Can you bring us a bottle of vodka and a shot glass?"

"Two," Knox interjects. "You have to play too."

"But I don't want to kiss you," I protest.

His eyes dance in quiet amusement. "That's a lie, and we both know it, Meggy."

Why does it turn me on, when he calls me on my bullshit? His eyebrows go up, and I shrug. "Fine. Order our damn dinner and we'll play your game, Knox."

Asher

She's furious. But I can see just how dilated her pupils are, the way her breasts are lifting with each breath—she's also turned on, even if she doesn't want to be. I sit back and nod at the waiting waitress. The girl vanishes and, a few minutes later, reappears with a bottle of Gray Goose and two shiny shot glasses.

Shit. When is the last time I did vodka shots? Why do I think it's a good idea now?

Oh. I don't. I'm not going to do many—because she's wrong. I do know her, and I'm damn well going to prove it.

"Favorite color?" she asks, and I laugh.

"Purple." She makes a face. "You're going to have to make them a little harder than that, pet."

"Fine. College major?"

"Psychology and business management—you double majored and graduated top of your class. You still have friends in both departments at Branton."

"You don't get extra tongue action because you have a long answer, Knox."

I almost choke on my tongue.

"Cats or dogs?"

"Neither, you prefer ferrets. Although, you do like puppies."

She sniffs, "I like kittens too."

"Everyone likes kittens. It doesn't mean we all want to adopt one."

She laughs, and I relax a little. If she's laughing, how mad can she be?

"Favorite vacation?"

I hesitate, thinking, and her smile turns into a self-satisfied smirk. "When you were a senior, you and your best friend drove from Branton to Orlando for a casting call during spring break. You worked as extras for a few days, and movies got into your blood. You stayed in cheap motels and ate greasy diner food, and when you got home, you avoided her for a month even though you adore her."

Her mouth forms a little 'o' of surprise, and I smile. "You talk, Meggy. And I listen."

"Clearly," she mutters, shifting in her seat.

"I haven't opened the bottle, Megs. Should we keep going?"

Her eyes narrow. "When did I lose my virginity?"

I lean back, trying to keep my breathing even. I can feel the waitress in the wings, but I want to answer this.

Except I don't know the answer.

"Prom." I finally say, because isn't that the cliché? Isn't that when girls typically give it up?

"Nope. I was sixteen, and it was right after Nik left home to move into the sorority house. I went to a party with her, and it just sorta happened."

I feel my gut hollow out. It just happened? What does that mean? Did it not mean anything? How could she let someone who didn't adore her touch her like that—and for her first time? The crack of the plastic on the vodka jars me back into the present. She spills a shot into the waiting glass and pushes it across the table to me.

"Drink up, Knox."

"You owe me four kisses," I say, and she inhales. Opens her mouth to say something, but I signal the waitress, and she moves forward with our appetizer as I take the first shot.

After the waitress moves away and we situate our plates, I pin Megan with a heavy stare. "Your turn. When did I graduate?"

"That's a trick question—you didn't. You dropped out before graduation and started working on a regular basis."

I cock my head—most people don't know I dropped out a few weeks before graduation. It was a move most people in my life said was idiotic, and I tended to agree, even if it was the break that led me to today.

Megan flushes. "Knowing your history is part of the job, Knox."

"Favorite book?"

"*The Name of the Wind.* Although, you'd probably tell the paps something like *Of Mice and Men.*"

I laugh, because it's true. She smirks and takes a bite of the shrimp scampi. A drop of garlic butter clings to her bottom lip, and I want to reach over and catch it with my own. I force myself to stay firmly in my own seat, and she smirks.

"So. You have two kisses."

Her expression takes on a slightly panicked expression, but she shrugs. "Next?"

"Which captain was my favorite?"

"Pine."

I smirk. "You just think so because we had drinks a few times. Picard was my favorite. Mum used to make me watch with her every time I took a sick day."

She tilts her head, "You loved her very much, didn't you?"

I close my eyes and reach for the vodka. I pour two and slide a shot to her. I need one—but then I usually do, when I think about Mum.

"She never wanted me to come here. She was convinced it would be a bad idea for me—that the way she raised me would be swallowed up by Hollywood."

"Was she right?"

Somehow, the conversation has veered away from our game, to things deeper than I think either of us expected.

"Yes. Sometimes. It's why I run, some days. I need to get away and remember the things she taught me, the things that make me her son."

She gasps, a tiny noise I don't think she intended to release, and I look at her.

"She would have liked you," I say, softly, brushing my fingertips over her hand. I wonder if she knows that it is the highest compliment I can pay someone.

"What is one place I want to see before I die?"

"Sydney," I say, promptly, not mentioning I will take the first role I'm offered with filming in Australia, just so I can take her there.

"Yours is Rio," She says, looking away as the waitress returns with our entrees.

My phone—the one she would be furious if she knew I had—buzzes against my leg and I almost reach for it. But I know who it will be, and I'm not ready to share this with Luca—not yet. So I close the bottle of vodka and change the subject.

We stay there for hours. Talking about nothing and everything, but the conversation shifts away from heavy topics, after that.

"How did you meet Luca? What's his deal?" I ask, after listening to another story about her roommates.

Her expression softens. "He was a good friend, when I desperately needed one. The best friend I could ask for."

"You slept with him," I say, and it's a statement rather than a question.

"No," she says, shaking her head. "Luca—he has to have Sun. It's not a bad thing—just his thing. And I've never been into sharing, so we've always been friends. I think he wanted more, but I...I just never wanted that."

I turn her words over in my head, trying to make sense of them, seeing Luca in a new light. She puts her fork down, the brownie we've been sharing almost completely gone.

"I'm going to the ladies room, and then I'll be ready to go."

I nod absently. As soon as she's gone, I grab my phone and dial quickly. Luca answers immediately.

"Your ignoring my texts," he says.

"And you're playing a dangerous game," I hiss back. "What is this? Is it some elaborate game your playing to get her in bed? She told me you like to share."

"Fuck." He sighs. "Look, English, don't overreact."

"How exactly do you think I should react?" I ask icily.

"What did you want me to say? That I love her and, by the way, I'm into threesomes? I just met you, man."

"And yet you sent her away with me."

"She needs this. Don't fool yourself into thinking I did this for anyone but Megan."

I shake my head. I don't know why he did this, and I don't have the energy to figure it out right now. Not when Megan will be back any second.

"I gotta go," I say abruptly.

I hang up and drop my head into my hands. What the hell does it mean? What does he want?

"Asher?"

I will never get tired of hearing my name on her lips. I love *Knox*, in her crisp tone that borders on exasperation. But when she softens enough to use *Asher*—that never fails to get me a little hard.

She's standing there, head cocked as she waits for me to respond. I shove all thoughts of Luca aside and stand.

Megan

I keep waiting, and he doesn't say anything. We walk through the cold night, and for the longest time, I think he's forgotten the kisses.

Nerves are strung tight in my belly, and I don't know if it's the dinner or the place or what he said about his mother. All I know is that I need something, rules be damned.

"You earned five kisses, you know."

The words fill the space between us, and I feel my cheeks heat. "You earned three," he says, a tease in his tone.

I did. But I can't use them. Can I?

I make an impatient sound and step away, ahead of him. I hear the soft whisper of satin, and then he grips my arm, pulling me around until I'm in his embrace without ever deciding that I want to be. His arms are around me, resting low on my hips, the tips of his fingers brushing the top of my ass. My hands come up, gripping his lapels, and I have a heartbeat to stare into his vibrant, blue eyes, and then his lips come down on mine.

They're as soft as they appear, a silky fullness that rubs across mine in a shallow kiss that lingers and slides, deepening without ever pulling away. His grip shifts on me, pulling my body tight against his, and I squirm against the press of his erection as he deepens the kiss, catching my lip with his teeth and sucking softly. I gasp, and his tongue slides against mine, an erotic velvety rub that has me aching for more.

91

I moan, and he makes a low noise, half growl, half groan, in the back of his throat, shifting to lift me. My legs come up and around his waist, my skirt riding up, and I have a heartbeat to wonder what the hell I'm doing before his tongue is retreating and he's sucking, lightly, the slightest pull, on mine. I want to scream, and I can't, I can't even breath. I need something—anything—more. My nails dig into his chest, and he shudders. My back hits the door. I slide down his body as I feel him fumbling. I catch his hand and I guide it where I want. He gasps when I let go, breaking the kiss finally, as his fingers trail over the skin of my thigh.

I go up on tiptoes, arching into his caress. "Don't stop." I beg, and I don't even care that I'm begging.

His gaze darkens, just a little, and then his fingers drift, lazily, up. I whimper when he brushes against me lightly, a fleeting touch that does more to aggravate than it does to soothe. "What do you want, pet?" he murmurs.

"Asher, please," I whimper, and his hand is there, brushing against my thong.

"Lace? So impractical," he says, a grin in his tone. I want to say something, but his finger is there, a soft pressure as he strokes me, and his lips are pressing against my neck, hot, open mouthed kisses that are driving me crazy. They aren't enough.

It's not enough.

I said it out loud. I must have. He pulls back, his gaze hot, and jerks my dress to the side. My breasts spill out, and I gasp as the cool air hits me. Then the warmth of his mouth covers me, and his tongue is twisting over my nipple. I shudder, and his hand moves, fingers dipping, dragging over me. I feel my orgasm coming, every nerve in my body tight, a taught coil of need focused on the two points he's touching me. I whimper, and he bites down, lightly, as his fingers thrust deep.

And everything explodes, a thin cry breaking free as my body tightens and lights dance behind my closed eyes. Euphoria and a wave of sleepiness slide over me as the orgasm eases. I shiver, slumped against the door. Knox straightens slowly, and I pry my eyes open to stare at him. He tucks my panties—when did he tear them?—into his pocket and adjusts my dress so I'm covered. As he opens the door to let me inside, and I have the first pangs of *what the hell*, he leans down, smelling of sex and male, and whispers in my ear, "That's one kiss, darling."

Asher

She's already reacting, already shutting down and retreating from me as we enter the house. Irrationally, I'm angry with her. I knew that this would happen. But after the brief intimacy and feeling her come apart, I'm not ready to let her go.

Still, something says this is for the best, so I give her space and let her retreat into her bedroom and shut the door behind her. Leaving me with a serious case of blue balls. And even though I understand her reasons and why she's running, I'm angry and frustrated and more than a little drunk. It's a bad combination.

Growling, I jerk my shirt over my head and stalk into my bedroom, throwing it onto the ground. My phone is a solid weight in my pocket, annoying me even further. Before I can figure out the consequences or why the hell I'm doing it, I'm dialing Luca's number.

All I know is that this man exploded into my life. He's her best friend, and it's clear that he wants her, so why the fuck is he helping me? What game is he playing? I hold the phone to my ear, and, as it rings, I have to wonder what I'm even going to say?

"Hello?"

"What are you doing?"

The question comes without preamble or artifice. He sighs. I can picture him, sprawled half naked in the big bed by himself. For some reason the picture, while lonely, doesn't disturb me as much as I expect. "Why are you doing this?" I demand.

"Do you trust that I love her?" he asks.

Of course I do, but that's the only thing I trust about him. "I know that you won't hurt her."

He laughs. It's bitter and mocking, a little bit hateful. But I can't figure out if it's directed at me or him.

"You know, she's my best friend. She's the only thing that keeps me sane. I'm watching her, and I'm watching you, and I'm watching what she does for that asshole she feels like she has to impress. You know what I see?"

I don't respond. There's nothing to say. I don't know, and I'm not sure I want to.

"She's losing herself. She's letting go of everything that makes her special and unique, beautiful and perfect. Everything that separates her from the city. She's letting it go because she feels like she has to to survive. And she's so hell-bent on proving herself, she doesn't even realize what's happening."

A long moment of quiet. As if he expects me to respond to that, but how do you respond to that? What do you even say? His words are ripping me to shreds. The more I think about it, the more I look back over the time I've spent with her, and I know it's true. Eventually, he says softly, "You asked me what I'm doing. You care about her. I care about her. And I'm trying my damnedest save her."

"From Kevin?" I ask.

"No," he says, so softly that I almost don't hear it. "I'm trying to save her from herself."

There's a long moment of silence as both of us absorb that. His goals and how I play into them. I still don't know, but for the first time tonight, I'm okay with that, because I believe him. He does care about her, and so do I.

"What happened today?" he asks.

Part of me doesn't want to tell him about the kiss. I don't want his memory there between us, but the truth is, Lucas has been between us since we arrived here. So I tell him, and I listen as his breathing gets deep. He's not even trying to hide that he's turned on.

I remember what she said about his sharing, and I wonder what will happen when we arrive in Las Vegas tomorrow.

Part of me wants to ask, but part of me is scared. I've never done this before—and I've done a lot. He takes away the option. "Get some sleep, English. You have a long drive tomorrow."

Luca

I sit staring at the phone after Asher hangs up.

I can picture them easily, him pressing her against the wall, her dress pulled aside. That's not what occupies my thoughts. Not completely.

I miss her. Which is irrational, because I saw her only a few days ago. But then, when it comes to Megan, I've never been the most rational person.

I'm not jealous. I know I'm not. I've never been the type to get jealous, and I knew when I told Asher to take her to that stupid villa that this would happen. Megan is very good at putting up walls and building rules and shielding herself against everything that she wants.

But she does want, and I knew that if she was given a little bit of space and a little bit of room to breathe away from Kevin, it was just a matter of time.

But she's there with him, and I'm here alone, and Sun's nowhere in sight and won't be for I don't know how long.

The worst part is I should miss Sun. I know I should, but I don't. I miss Megan. And Asher, the stupid English idiot with all of his uppity manners and his smiles. I can understand why she can't get past him. I grab my phone again and send a quick message.

Nothing that'll freak her out. Just a quick reminder that I'm still here—he might have just brought her to an orgasm that made her knees weak and I would pay good money to watch, but I'm still here. Me. Her best friend. The one who rescued her.

I hope she still needs me.

I turn it off after sending. I don't want to deal with the apologies or the guilt that I know she's feeling.

I hit the lights and lie down. As the city comes to life around me, I lie in the darkness, staring at the ceiling, and I wonder what will tomorrow bring.

Sweet Ruin

Chapter Eight

Megan

"I love Las Vegas."

It's the first thing I've said all morning, and it feels almost like confession of sorts as I stare at Asher from across the table.

Irrationally, I wonder when he'll kiss me again. Nope, wrong train of thought. That's not what I'm supposed to be thinking at breakfast today, after I did something incredibly stupid. Something I'm not going to repeat.

Right. Because if I keep repeating that over and over, maybe someday—today, tomorrow, next year—it'll be true.

I clear my throat. "What are you looking at in Vegas? Aren't we supposed to be getting on the road on Monday?"

Knox drops the paper and gives me a steady stare. "Remember how Kevin's been trying to get hold of you?"

I straighten. "Yeah, what about it?"

"He might not be happy. But it's not your fault, and he knows it's not your fault, so don't worry too much, okay?"

Very slowly and very precisely, I set down my spoon. Knox edges away from the table, expression wary. "What the hell did you do, Knox?"

"I said don't be mad."

"You lied to get me here. And then you seduce me against my damn door. And now there's something going on with my job, the job that I take very seriously! And you're telling me not to get upset? You better explain yourself right now, or I swear to God I will walk out the door and you will never see me again."

He winces, a defeated expression coming across his face. And then, with a heavy sigh, he tells me.

I don't want to believe him. It's been forty-five minutes since he told me about fight with Kevin, his ultimatum and Kevin's retaliation. And I want to believe he's lying. But I know my uncle, and this is just the exact jackass bullshit that he would pull.

He's been jealous since he gave me the client. Me. The little niece that he didn't want to work with, the one he didn't want to give a job, and the only one who can keep the biggest client happy. I zip my bag with an angry twist of my hand and stalk out to the living room.

Knox is standing there, worried expression stitching his brow. "Relax, Asher. I'm over it. Mostly. Okay, not at all, but I'm not mad at you. Much."

His eyebrows goes up, and he smirks. "Is that supposed to reassure me?"

"Did it work?"

"Not at all."

I sniff, "Then no. It wasn't."

He laughs, like he's supposed to.

That's me. Doing my job, keeping the talent happy. Except it's not my job anymore, is it?

"Hey, Megs?"

"Yeah?"

"It's going to be okay. I don't know how, but it will be. I promise."

Despite my anger and the generally fucked-up situation, I have to admit my heart melts just a little bit. Because he's trying—he's trying to save me, and nobody does that. Nobody but Luca.

Suddenly, the desire to see my best friend is overwhelming. I grab my bag. "Come on. It's a long drive, and I want to go."

The way he's looking at me, Knox knows something is going on. But all those times I let his bullshit slide finally pay off. He doesn't comment on my suddenly erratic behavior, just takes the bag for me and leads the way out of the little villa.

Not terribly surprising, Knox has coffee waiting in the car. I settle into my seat and take a sip and try very hard to turn my mind off for the next five hours.

Asher

She's asleep and has been for a while. I'm okay with that. I was a little worried when she first found out what Kevin did and why I abducted her.

Abduct is a strong word. It's not exactly the one that I would've chosen. I like to think of it as I borrowed her for a few days.

Whatever. She's okay with it.

Okay, she's still pissed.

We hit the city limits, and I turn the radio down, grabbing my phone. Luca, not surprisingly, answers on the first ring.

"Where are you?" he asks.

"We're in the city, but we just got here. It's going to be a while. Are you still at your shoot?"

"Yeah. I should be done in an hour. Just head to the hotel."

I find myself nodding before I remember he can't see me. Idiot. But I feel like he deserves some kind of warning. Even if he's working, I need to tell him. "Luca, she knows."

"How the hell did she find out?" he asks.

"Well, she was going to find out some point. I mean how else was I going to get her to Vegas?"

He's quiet for a long time, and then, "Dude, I got to go. They're calling me back. Just take her to the hotel. It's room 1159." He hangs up quickly, before I can respond. I curse.

"Was that Luca?" she asks, her voice rough with sleep.

I would kill to be the first one to hear her voice every morning. Does that make me a little bit maladjusted? Probably. Am I okay with that? Yes.

"What's wrong? Why did Luca sound so pissed?"

"I think he wanted to be the one to tell you about Kevin."

"He knows?" she says, her voice going shrill and losing that gravelly sleep tone.

"Yeah. I sort of ran into him when I was leaving Kevin's office, and yeah."

I cringe, cursing myself. What is it about this girl that turns me into a babbling idiot? She gives me a disbelieving sort of look. "You're just now telling me this?"

"But you get to yell at him too, right?"

She glares and I hurry on. "If you're going to yell at both of us, don't you think it'd be better to wait and do it together? It saves you some time and me from getting it twice."

She tries to maintain the angry stare, but I see her lips twitching to a smile. "Most people don't mind getting it twice," she mutters.

I snort. "That's what she said."

She laughs, the carefree sound filling the tiny space of the car and making my heart jump. Dude, I've turned into such a girl.

"So where are we going?" she asks, leaning her head back. The heater in the car is turned all the way up, and it's brought a flush to her cheeks. Red curls are slipping out of the messy ponytail. I want to catch one and tug at it.

I keep my hands firmly on the wheel and shrug one shoulder. "He's staying at the Luxor. We can go there, or do something else."

Her head tilts back, neck craning to see the skyline. "Can we go to the Stratosphere and ride the coaster? The one where you dangle eight hundred feet above the strip?"

I choke. "Seriously?"

She laughs again, leans back against her seat. "No, not seriously. I mean, I do want to ride it, but Luca would be really upset if I went without him. Do you mind?"

A wave of relief sweeps over me. "No. That's fine, we can wait," I say, my voice oddly high. She gives me a slightly suspicious look, but doesn't push for more.

"So, the problem is going to be that, if we go out anywhere, you're likely to be recognized and mobbed, and nobody really wants that."

I slide a glance her way. This is by far the only time she's suggested not taking me in public. And since it is a hotel room waiting on the other end of this trip—"Are you trying to get me in bed?" I ask.

Color flood her cheeks. She looks away. "Not everything is about sex, Asher."

I laugh, "Yeah, darling, it is."

It kicks off an argument that lasts until we're almost at the hotel, and I'm okay fighting with her. I'm okay with just about anything as long as she's happy and smiling.

"Do I need to go and get us a key?" she asks, staring up at the Luxor.

"Yeah, you probably better, I think, if you want to avoid a mob scene."

She rolls her eyes. "No one knows you're going to be here. I doubt they're just lying around in the lobby for you."

"But you don't know that they're not," I point out reasonably. "Besides, it doesn't matter if they're waiting for me. When they see me, it'll devolve into chaos. You know that."

"Fine. Wait here."

She startles me, leaning in and dropping a quick kiss on my lips before she hops out of the car and starts inside. I think I might like this new playful side of her.

Megan

There's a line to the reception desk, so I wait patiently and think about what I just did.

Kissing Ash was such a bad idea. The longer we're away from LA and the more time I spend with him, the more I forget why. And it's not like it can affect my job anymore. Fuck, what am I going to do about that? Panic closes in on me, and I breath, trying to focus on forcing a smile for the receptionist as she calls me up.

"Hi. I'm meeting a friend. He's already got a room and put me on the list?"

She gives me a warm smile and looks at a computer. "Name and room number?"

I rattle off the information, and a few minutes later I'm holding a shiny plastic key.

It occurs to me that we still have to get Asher through crowded hotel lobby, so I look at the lady and ask, "Where is your gift shop?"

She points me in the general direction, and I make my way there. It's predictably tacky, filled with overpriced snacks and hats and sunglasses.

Exactly what I need.

I pick the most ridiculous hat I can find and an obnoxious pair of sunglasses. I make my way back out to the car. Knox is waiting, an expectant look on his face.

"Here," I say tossing the bag to him.

He looks at it like it might be a bomb. "What is this?" he asks.

"Just put it on," I say in a huff.

"This is a really bad disguise," he says.

It is. The hat and glasses do nothing to disguise the way his face looks, a strong jawline the begs for kisses. The glasses do hide his baby blues. And the hat casts enough of a shadow that there's a trace of doubt. And really, all I need is a shadow of a doubt.

"Quit bitching and let's go."

He grins, and we both climb out of the car.

Everything is fine, until he reached the elevators. A group of people lingers there waiting for the elevators to descend, including several teenage girls. I can feel Asher stiffening, reacting next to me. Without thinking, I reach out and grab his hand. His grip on me is painfully tight, as if I'm a lifeline, the tether keeping him here. For some reason, it doesn't bother me as much as it should.

"Keep it together," I whisper. He steps behind me, dropping the arm around my waist, holding me too him. I have moment to think *what the fuck* before his lips descend on the back of my neck.

And I'm on sensory overload, unable to think beyond the fact that he's kissing me and I don't want him to stop.

I hear the girls behind us giggling and the murmur of people around us—I think someone even whistles—but I'm lost in the press of his lips on the back of my neck, his hands hot and low on my waist. I shiver, and the elevator dings, the doors sliding open.

Without releasing me, he nudges us into motion, positioning us in the back of the elevator. "Tell them which floor," he orders, his voice husky in my ear, tongue darting out and licking over my earlobe.

"Which floor?" someone calls.

"Eleven," I say, a few other people chiming in. I can't see them—Asher is bent over me, the bill of his ball cap obscuring us both. He twists me a little, until I face him. His eyes are still hidden behind those damn glasses, but his lips are soft and fuller than I've seen them, and I have a heartbeat to realize that's because of me, and then he's kissing me.

This man could make a fortune at a kissing booth, I think before I lose track of rational thought.

Asher

She's soft and pliant, a warm arch of skin and curves pressing against every inch of me. Her lips open on the softest sigh, and my hands leave the delectable curve of her waist, coming up to twist into her hair and hold her in place as I deepen the kiss.

It was supposed to be a diversion—just something to make people think about something other than who I am.

It's become so much more, and I don't want to stop.

Her tongue darts out, rubbing against mine, and I have to. I have to pull back because I want to fuck her, and I'm not going to push her here, not in a crowded elevator on the way to her best friend's hotel room.

I kiss her once more, a soft press against the top of her head, and she shivers against me. The elevator slows, my stomach doing that swoopy thing as it pauses at floor eleven. I take her hand and pull her off the elevator.

As the door begins to slide shut, one of the teen girls says, fervently, "God, I want someone to kiss me like that."

I tug my glasses off and twist to wink at her.

The expression of startled wonder is priceless, probably the highlight of her vacation.

Megan is staring at me, her face a mix of bemused tolerance .

"You really are an idiot," she says, and I laugh. For the first time, I look around. The halls are long, a repeating pattern in beige and scarlet. It's garish and dizzying. "Apparently the décor budget was used downstairs," I say dryly.

She rolls her eyes, and I reach down, grabbing her bag as she leads the way down the long hall to room 1159.

It's a modest room—the kind a mid-level actor would rate. But there's a spacious bathroom and a large bed and—

"Why is there only one bed?" I ask, my voice a little uneven.

Her cheeks color, and she looks away. "Luca and I usually share. We're pretty comfortable in each other's space, you know, and he knows my limits."

I stare at her for a long minute. Debate telling her the truth about her beloved best friend.

"You remember that, before we left, I knew you had limits? And yet, I just kissed you in the elevator and I already want to kiss you again? I want to strip you bare and see everything that I touched last night, and go down on you until you're screaming. That's well past your limits, isn't it?"

Her eyes go wide, and her breath is coming in short little pants. Her tongue darts out, licking over her lips, and I groan.

"Luca doesn't do one on one," she says, looking back at the bed. "And I don't think you're into sharing."

I raise an eyebrow. "Luca seems to think that's *your* hang-up."

"What, did y'all discuss it while I was in the other room?" she asks, her voice turning a little tart.

"Yes."

Her mouth falls open, her eyes going wide. I look away—I need to step back, get her on comfortable footing. Or she's going to wind up naked, under me.

"You want to shower first?" I ask, taking a mental and physical step back. Her brows stitch in confusion, and then she nods, giving her travel clothes a slightly disgruntled look.

"Yeah."

She turns without another word, stalking into the bathroom and letting the door slam shut behind her. I text Luca quickly.

Me: We're here.

He doesn't respond, and as the water turns on, I sit down on the bed. Listening to her shower while I sit alone in the next room is a special kind of torture. One I wouldn't be indulging in if I had my way. But I've waited this long, and Luca will be here soon and…what? What will happen then?

My phone lights up.

Luca: Dinner in or out?

Me: In.

I can almost see the other man thinking, and I follow the text with another.

Me: I'm tired, and want to avoid a riot if possible. I can't make out with Meg every time a teen girl happens to be around.

Luca: ??

Me: Nothing. The elevators provided a uniquely difficult situation for avoiding recognition.

Luca: I can't leave you two alone for a minute, can I?

I laugh. There is something so amused and exasperated in the question, I can't help but laugh.

Luca feels like an old friend—someone who fits into my life like he's carved a niche and made a place for himself there, instead of having met me only a week or so ago. No one ever feels like that. It's disconcerting.

Luca: She's going to want to go out before we leave.

Me: I know. The little idiot wants to ride the damn X-Scream. You can take her tomorrow.

Luca: Pussy. I'll grab something for dinner. Be there soon.

Luca

I stop and grab sushi, salads, and a piece of prime rib for Asher. I could order room service, but this is better—and Megan's favorite. I'm anxious, and I don't like it. It's a feeling I'm not used to. I don't usually care what people think or if I'm going to get laid. But this isn't people—it's Megan. And that makes all the difference in the world.

I stand outside our room for a long minute, getting up the nerve to push the door open. I can hear them talking inside, her laughter and his low rumble. After I open the door, things will change, and I don't know how. I don't know if they're ready for it.

Too late to back out now.

Both of them sort of freeze when I open the door. Asher looks at me like he has never seen me before, and Megan gives me a brilliant smile and hurries across the room to wrap her arms around me. "I missed you," she says, her voice soft in my ear.

I squeeze her tight before I release her, and she steps back. Immediately, I feel a sense of loss, and I want to pull her back against me. Her gaze is going between me and Asher, her expression a little bit hesitant.

There's an awkward pause, all of us wondering what to do next. "I have food," I say.

She grins and takes the bag from me, twisting away to sway to the little table. I eye Knox as she opens the food, watching his gaze following her. I shift, and his eyes shoot back to me. I lift an eyebrow, and he smirks, a blatant disregard.

It makes me angry, the fact that he can dismiss me so easily.

He forgets, Megan has been mine far longer than he's been in her life, and she's comfortable with me.

Sometimes, being a friend can be a real benefit.

I follow her across the room and step up behind her. She goes stiff for a moment, then relaxes against me. "Can I help, lovely girl?" I ask.

She flashes me a quick smile and kisses my cheek. "No. Oh, we need ice?"

I snake a hand around her waist, stealing a crouton and letting my fingers skim over her hip, the soft v of her thigh curving into her body, and she shivers. Her eyes, when they come up to mine, are filled with hunger and questions. I've seen this look in her eyes so many times before, and I've always stepped back, always let her have the comfort of our friendship because she didn't want what I was offering.

I step into her space, and her breath catches, her eyes going wide and startled. I lean over, letting my breath brush against her skin, and I can feel the softness of her hair and the warmth of her skin. It would be so easy, to twist just a little and kiss her.

Easy, and not what she needs. Yet. So I pluck the ice bucket from the table and straighten with a small smile. I grin at Knox as I turn, a cocky smirk as I head out the door.

"I'll go with you," he says, shifting off the bed. Meg goes still, watching us with big, concerned eyes. I flash her a smile, and her shoulders relax a little.

Knox is quiet as we walk through the hallways, and I'm thankful that casino hotel hallways don't get nearly as much action as their gaming floors—we're unobserved.

At the little cubicle, the sound of the ice machine buzzing around us, I finally look at him.

"What?"

"You want her," he says, without heat. It's not an accusation, it's an observation.

I nod. "Yes. I do."

"And I want her."

I take a deep breath, nervous, and force myself to meet his gaze. "Yes."

"Where does that leave us?"

I don't want to spell it out. I don't want to explain to him what I want. Or why. Why can't we just get drunk and fuck and deal with the awkward bullshit in the morning?

"Why does it have to be either or?" I say, my voice low. I glance up at him and find his expression thoughtful. I shiver under the weight of his gaze and look away. I'm not used to someone else having the upper hand in a relationship. It makes things hella hard.

"She wants both of us," I say, turning away and shoving the bucket under the ice dispenser.

I feel his motion a second before I feel his breath, his voice a murmur in my ear.

"And do you? Do you want us both?"

I shudder and let the bucket go, turning to face him. He's close, and his height is almost even with mine, making this strangely intimate.

"Yes," I say, without hesitation.

His eyes dilate, and he inhales sharply. His lips hover, a few inches from mine, and I want to close the gap, and I want to shove him away.

"Fuck," I mutter, pulling back. Asher's expression stutters into shock. "I'm too sober, Knox. I won't lie—of course, I want you. But I'm too sober to try and seduce a straight man. I'm not that desperate. I won't interfere, when it comes to you and her. All I ask that you do the same."

He hesitates, and the ice machine comes to life, startling us. I jerk the bucket free and raise an eyebrow. He nods. "Deal."

I let out the breath I'm holding and grin at him. He follows me through the halls back to our room. I tap on the door. As I wait for Megs to open it, Asher leans in again, his breath brushing over the nape of my neck. and whispers, "Order tequila, Luca. See what happens."

I stare at him, stunned, as he steps past me into the room.

Chapter Nine

Asher

Dinner is not as awkward as I expect. Megan and Luca chatter comfortably, and I sit to the side, watching with a slight smile.

There is a subtle game being played out here, with half glances and shifting eyes and a bottle of tequila I haven't opened. Is drinking the right idea?

"What do y'all want to do tonight?" she asks. Luca's gaze darts to mine—I noticed the slip as well.

Megan is careful to keep her accent controlled—stress and comfort brings it out in full force. I'm betting that this particular instance is brought on by stress more than a level of comfort we're not used to seeing from her.

"We could go to a club," Luca says.

Her eyes light up, and she bounces in her chair. "Dancing?"

"As much as I'd love to see you dance, pet, I think going out is a good way to incite a riot."

She frowns, nibbling on her lower lip. "Good point. Annoying, though."

I laugh. "Usually you love my publicity."

"Usually, it's my job to," she counters. "Which we still need to discuss."

Luca catches her hand, tugging her away from the little table with the remains of our dinner and over to the bed. "Can we discuss it tomorrow, lovely girl? I've missed you, and I just want to enjoy a little time together before we start fighting."

He sits back on the bed, drawing her down with him until she's sitting between his legs, back propped against him. I watch her snuggle against his chest, and it hits me that this is normal for them. They have a casual intimacy that boggles my mind—she doesn't keep him at an arm's length the way she always has me. I don't understand it, and I'm honest enough to admit that it stings, a little.

"Pick a movie," Luca says, meeting my eyes. He holds out the remote, and I take it, shifting in my chair. I pick a recent romance that I remember her saying she wanted to watch.

It occurs to me that romance, while she's sitting in another man's arms, is probably a bad idea, but her eyes are warm and pleased when she realizes what I've picked. I smile at her and sit back in the chair. We only get five minutes into the movie before she shifts forward and to the side, grabbing a pillow and placing it on her leg. "You don't have to sit over there," she says.

I hesitate, staring at her. My gaze flicks up, nervously, to Luca. His expression is patient and waiting. He'll accept whatever I do, but I know he wants me. Do I want to open this door?

Without letting myself think too much, I settle across the bed, propping my head on the side of her thigh. She sighs, and the room goes quiet as we watch the movie.

Megan

I can't focus. It's a damn shame, too; I've been excited about this movie. But as the characters flirt and dance around each other on screen, I'm pinned between Luca and Asher, overly aware of both. Asher's head is a solid pressure on my leg, and Luca is firm pressure behind me, his hand splayed across my belly. I tilt my head slightly, and the fingers of his other hand comb through my hair, a slow, steady stroke that makes me want to arch into the caress and purr. He presses a kiss to the top of my hair, and I shift, a minute motion that causes Asher to lift his head.

Without thinking, I tug him back down, my fingers working down to his neck, rubbing softly. I expect him to react, to turn to me, but he doesn't. He goes soft and pliant, which in turns makes me relax against Luca. His hand on my belly shifts softly, a gentle caress. I twist my head to look at him, but he's watching the movie. I refocus, and my breath catches as the couple on screen makes out, the hero pinning her against the wall.

It reminds me too much of the kiss at the villa, which I shouldn't be thinking about.

Luca's hand moves again, an unmistakable brush of his thumb against the underside of my breast. I'm not wearing a bra, and his hand stills as he realizes that. I twist again, and this time, his eyes are on me, blazing with heat and need. I shift, and we both gasp as his hand cradles my breast. His head dips down, but he hesitates, his gaze questioning.

Without thinking about the consequences, I pull him down to me.

His lips are hot, and dry, and firm, brushing over mine like he's kissed me a thousand times—or stared at my mouth long enough to memorize it. I whimper into the kiss as he sweeps into my mouth with a strong stroke, tongue sliding along mine. His finger brushes across my nipple and I groan, arching into him.

Asher's head lifts, and I feel the bed shifts. Aware suddenly, I break the kiss, and twist to stare at him.

"Don't stop," he says, softly, staring at us. Luca inhales sharply, and I almost protest, but Luca's hands are tugging at my breast, and I can't stop the whimper rising in my throat. His lips are playing across the back of my neck, kissing and sucking and nipping, as his fingers circle. He bites down as he pinches my nipple, and I shudder, almost arching off the bed. I want more—

I twist in his arms, coming up on my knees as I straddle him. Our groans fill the room as I grind against his erection, his big hands cradling my hips and guiding me. I tug at my shirt impatiently, and Asher's hands catch the hem, helping pull it off. I look at him, startled. His gaze is hot and needy, and I want to kiss him, kiss away the stich in his brow.

Wet heat envelopes one nipple as fingers tug the other, and I make a noise, somewhere between sob and scream, grinding down on Luca's erection. He nips me, lightly, and pulls back. His lips are glossy, and I want to yank him back down, but he's looking past me, to Asher.

"Do you want this?"

I shudder when Knox nods. Both men stare at me, and I can't remember why this is a bad idea. I nod slowly, and Asher shifts up on his knees, pressing against me as he kisses the nape of my neck.

"Lose the pants, pet."

I shiver at the hint of command in his tone, and hurry to do as he says. I feel a heartbeat of hesitation, but they're sitting side by side, dark and golden and so damn gorgeous I want to cry. Without letting myself think anymore, I wiggle out of my sleep shorts, dropping my lace boy shorts with them.

Both men go still, and Luca lets out a shaky breath, reaching for me. "You're gorgeous, lovely. So perfect." His finger brushes over my smooth mound, dipping down to flit over my clit and slide through my slit.

"Is she wet?" Asher asks, his voice hoarse. I shiver as he stares at me, his hands clenched, watching my best friend finger me.

"Yes," I whimper, and arch into Luca's touch.

"Lie down, sweetheart," Asher says. The boys shift to the side, and I stretch out between them. Luca's fingers are still caressing me, a light pressure that isn't nearly enough. I whimper, and he leans down, kissing me. I lose myself in that kiss, in the slide of his tongue against mine, the nip of his teeth, and the butterfly soft strokes of his fingers on my breasts.

And then I go rigid, feeling Asher kissing his way down my torso. I pull back and stare up at Luca, frantic.

"Shh, hush, lovely. We've got you. Let him have a taste, sweetheart." I look down as Asher licks me, his tongue moving over my slit in a deliberate caress, and I groan, a low broken noise. He smirks at me, an angel on his knees, and bends his head to focus on my pussy.

"You have no idea how long I've wanted this," Luca breathes, peppering kisses down my throat and over my breasts. "Or how hot it is, to see him going down on you. It's so fucking sexy."

I groan, arching into the hands and tongue working me over, and Asher chuckles. "Think she likes the dirty talk, Luc."

"Do you?" Luca asks, and I scream as Asher's finger slides deep into my pussy. Asher sucks on my clit, and I writhe. "You like me talking to you while he finger fucks you, Megan? Do you like the idea of me watching while you give him head?"

"Yes," I gasp, so turned on I can barely breathe. "Please, Luca."

"What do you need, lovely?" he asks, and I whimper. I don't know, and I can't ask, and I need something. Asher shifts, adding a second finger in my pussy, and Luca fondles my breasts, leaning over to nip at me. Sensation coils tighter, and I scream as the orgasm hits me, slamming into me and throwing me into a maelstrom of sensation.

Luca

I've wanted this since the first day, but nothing—none of my fantasies—will ever live up to the reality of Megan falling apart under my hands. She whimpers and twitches as the orgasm sweeps through her, her eyes closed. Asher sits up slowly, and I catch his gaze. His eyes are still wild with lust, and I shiver.

Megan isn't the only one who needs release.

Slowly, giving him time to react and pull away, I lean forward. His eyes are a tiny bit wary, but he doesn't stop me as I hook a hand around his neck and tug him lightly toward me.

He tastes like her, his lips still wet. I kiss him lightly, at first, and he doesn't pull back. Tentatively, I run my tongue over the closed seam of his lips, and he opens with a soft sigh, one hand clenching on my shoulder as I deepen the kiss.

And he lets me, tongue flirting with mine in a subtle play that does nothing to ease my hard on.

When I pull back, aware that neither of us will go any further than this tonight, I catch Megan's eyes, drowsy but warm.

"Don't stop because of me, boys," she says, stretching. I laugh, and lean down to peck her lips. Asher smirks and rises from the bed, finding her shirt. She wiggles into it and slides under the covers with a yawn.

"I'm sleepy," she says, and Asher slides into bed, cradling her to him as she drifts of to sleep. And somehow, despite the raging hard on, I make myself focus on the movie still playing on the screen.

Chapter Ten

Asher

"So we need to decide what to do," Megan says abruptly. It's been a tense morning, the intimacy of last night gone in the garish light of morning. Luca isn't looking at me—which might be because I shut down when he caught me jerking off this morning before Megan woke up.

Kissing him wasn't something I had planned, and I don't know what to do now.

It was easy, being with her, even with the murmuring presence of Luca. But what did that kiss mean? And did I really want to go there?

I shake my head and shrug. "We're going to Branton, right? Didn't your guy come through for the part?"

"He did. But you forget—I don't have a job. I can't just ignore the fact that Kevin wants my head on a plate."

"Do you think," Luca interjects from where he's shaving, "that he'll change his mind about you if you do come back?"

"Bear in mind you'll be going back without me. I can't right now, Meggy."

She sighs, annoyed. "You had the whole weekend." She staring at me like she's never seen me.

How do I explain to her that it's not enough? That after months of time in the city I need more than just days? "Meg, you said—"

She inhales sharply. "I know. I know what it said."

Something occurs to me, and I frown. "Do you not want to be with us?"

I see Luca stiffen across the room and realize what I said. Well shit, I didn't mean to let that slip.

"Is that what you think? It has nothing you do with us. It's my job. Luca, you know how much this means to me. You can't just disappear for a month." Megan protests.

"But going back won't solve anything, either," he says patiently.

"So what do you think that I should do?" she asks.

"I think I've been telling you for year to quit and start your own agency."

I jerk around, staring. Luca meets my gaze steadily for a second before it swings back to Megs.

"I can't go into business against my uncle. You know that."

"I know that I would follow if you open your own agency. I know that Luca would follow you," I say, bring my weight behind him.

Megan's eyes narrow. "Is this something he talked about to you?" she asks.

"No. But it's a logical step. Sweetheart, you're good at your job, and he treats you like shit. Why not?"

"So you think I should take his biggest client and my ex-roommate and run away for a month and come back to start my own agency. Is that the general plan you have?"

Luca nods. "That pretty much sums it up."

"Wait," I say, "you want to come with us."

For the first time Luca looks nervous. "Are you okay with that?"

I hesitate. "I don't know," I answer honestly.

Megan is watching us, her expression narrow and thoughtful. "Why don't we not decide right now?" she suggests. "Why don't I go out and find some food and some clothes for Asher, and Luca, you come with me?"

I feel a flash of jealousy—because he can go with her and I'm relegated to this damn room. I open my mouth to protest, and Megan shakes her head. "Not a good idea, and you know it. We can't afford for you to be exposed here—and until we figure this out"—she motions to the three of us—"you can't be seen with us. The tabloids would have a field day."

I know she's right, even I'm not incredibly happy about it. "What about Luc? People know his face."

She snorts. "People know his abs. And I'm seen with him all the time—I was his roommate, remember? It's the trifecta I'm worried about." She hesitates, crouching next to me. I like her at that level. I shove the thought down immediately— it's not going to do anyone any good right now.

"This isn't about last night," she murmurs, and I nod, even though it feels like it is. I can't get jealous—she isn't mine, and I told him I wouldn't cock-block. I stand abruptly. "I'm going to get a shower. I'll see you when you get back."

Megan's eyes are worried, and I drop her gaze, skirting her to head to the bathroom. Luca is blocking me, leaning almost lazily against the wall.

"Meggy, go downstairs. I'll meet you—I need to talk to Asher."

There is a second of deliberation, and his gaze goes past me, to where she's standing. His smile gentles, a little. "Go, lovely girl. I'll be right there."

She nods, grabbing her purse and cell phone before leaving in a puff of perfume and annoyed indignation. I stare at Luca as she lets the door shut behind her.

He doesn't move when we're alone, and I shift, annoyed. "What do you want?" I snap. "She's waiting."

"I've been clear about what I want," he says, finally looking up at me, and I shiver. The expression in his gaze is blatant.

"You can't do that," I say weakly.

"What?" he asks, voice soft.

"You can't just put it out there like that—that's not the way things are done."

Luca laughs, pushing off the wall at last. He crowds me, and I want to step back, but I can't bring myself to move. His eyes dilate a little, and he murmurs, "I'm done playing games, English. I thought you didn't like them. Was I wrong?"

He waits, a heartbeat or two, for my response, and then steps toward the door. "Would you follow her, if she left Kevin's agency?"

I go still—that's what he wants to know? I nod. "Of course. She's brilliant, Luca. I don't want anyone else working on my career."

He flashes me a quick smile and opens the door. Pauses. "This isn't worth being jealous over, Ash. You need to decide if you can be with us without jealousy."

"And if I can't?"

"Then this won't work. Jealousy doesn't belong in any relationship," he says, and then the door swings shut behind him.

Luca

By the time I reach the ground floor, my hands have steadied. Megan isn't near the elevator banks, but I'm not worried. I follow the scent of coffee and find her, head bent over her phone, as she stands by a post. I slide an arm around her waist, and she leans into me without looking up. "I ordered you a chai."

I press a kiss to her forehead, "Thanks, lovely."

She doesn't pull away—I'm not sure if that's because she's absorbed in the morning news, or because she's comfortable with me after last night. Either way, I'll take it. I hold her as she scans the tabloid sites, chewing her lip and muttering.

When the barista calls Megan's name, I shift away and retrieve our coffees. She shoves the phone into her purse and takes her latte.

My girl has her priorities straight—work will wait for fresh coffee.

"So, you want to come with us," she says, stirring sugar into the creamy coffee.

I nod. "Is that okay?"

"What's going on here?"

I shrug, trying to keep my heartbeat steady. "We're having fun, right?"

"Sun said you moved out," she says quietly.

Shit. I expel a slow breath and twist to look at her. I knew Sun would say *something*, but I didn't realize it would be that extreme. She's staring at me, a worried line between her eyes. I want to kiss that line away, but I know she won't tolerate it. Not right now.

"Talk to me, Luca," she says firmly. I nod. Without speaking, I lead her to a bench off the corridor. It's away from the gaming floor and the café, giving us an odd sort of privacy.

She sits down, her bag to one side, and I stretch my legs out, taking a cautious sip of my coffee.

"Did y'all fight?" she asks, her voice softening a little. I love when it does this and I get a hint of that southern drawl I adore.

I shake my head. "No. Nothing like that. We were just going in different directions, and I didn't want her to miss out on something real with Pablo because she was waiting on me."

"She loves you, Luca."

"Sun loves me like a brother," I say, shaking my head. Megan's eye brows shoot up, and I remember the time she came home to find me and Sun and a little brunette gymnast naked in the living room. "Ok," I amend, "not quite a brother."

"You've been with her for years."

I huff a sigh. "Meg, she's not what I want. She hasn't been what I want for almost two years. She knows that—it's why she started dating Pablo to begin with."

"But you didn't just break things off and leave Pablo a clear path. You moved out—you told her you were leaving California."

She flicks an anxious look at me, and I take a deep breath, understanding. "I need to leave for a while—it's one reason I want to go with you and Asher. I've been honest about what I want from you both."

She blinks and looks away, into her coffee. "And if I don't want that? Are you going to walk away from me like you did Sun?"

Pain hits me, like a fist. I stand abruptly and walk away from her. I fish my valet ticket out and hand it to the boy, trying to get a grasp on my temper. I can feel her walking up behind me, a silent presence as I wrangle with my anger.

Finally, I turn to her. "Are you fucking serious? Do you really think I would do that?"

Apparently I'm not as in control as I hoped. She heaves a tired sigh and comes close, setting her coffee down on the valet desk and wrapping her arms around me in a tight hug.

"I don't think anything—I don't know what to think. I'm nervous and I'm scared. I love you—and I had a lot of fun last night. But I want you in my life more than I want you in my bed. Does that make sense?"

I glance around, taking in the curious stares we're drawing. Even in Vegas, a girl who looks as effortlessly gorgeous as Megan will garner a few double takes when she talks about her sex life. I draw her away, toward a quiet corner, while we wait for the car.

"This doesn't have to be an either or, Megs. I don't want to just become a fuck buddy. I haven't pushed for this, not in the eighteen months we've known each other. I value what we have too much to risk losing you. But I want more than just a lunch every week or so. I want *you*, Megan."

Chapter Eleven

Megan

I take a deep breath and open the door to the hotel room. Asher's got the TV on, muted, and he sprawls across the bed. His eyes are closed, his chest rising in a steady rhythm. I pause in the doorway and smile, staring at him. Luca crowds against my back, carrying a few bags with clothes and some toiletries. Most of our purchases are still in the car downstairs.

"That's a damn pretty picture," Luca murmurs near my ear.

"Quit drooling," I tease. "Get packed."

He drops a kiss on the curve of my neck and steps away, pulling out the beat up duffle bag I've seen him carry everywhere since I moved in with him.

I tune him out as I crawl onto the bed, straddling Asher's prone form. I lean down slightly, brushing a butterfly soft kiss over his lips. Ash stirs, a tiny bit, and I apply a hint of pressure against his lips. He groans, a low, deep noise that sets my blood on fire, and his hands come up, clenching on my hips, hard. I will have bruises, tomorrow. As he deepens the kiss, his tongue darting out and delving past my lips, I find I don't care. I don't care about anything but him kissing me.

Silence fills the room, the only sound the brush of cloth and lips and the soft sigh I can't help but release, as his lips leave mine, traveling down, following the slope of my neck until he hits the top of my t-shirt. He growls and jerks at my shirt, his hands sliding under and up. I moan, arching into the caress, and Luca clears his throat.

Blinking slowly, I sit up. I know what I look like, my hair a mess, my lips full and pout, my nipples pressing against the thin shirt material.

"Don't rip her clothes, dude. We need to get out of here today, and I'm not going shopping again."

Despite the bracing words, he's smiling. I stick my tongue out, and go up on my knees, swinging off Asher with a deliberate little wiggle. "He's right, unfortunately. Get dressed, Knox. We need to hit the road."

Asher props himself up on an elbow. "Where are we going?"

I smirk and lean back down to kiss him quickly. "Branton, babe."

His eyebrows inch up, and I grin. "Come on. I want to get on the road."

I inch away from him and collide with Luca. His hands are hot on my hips, and he steadies me as I stumble. I lean into him briefly. Then pull away. "None of that. Pack."

"Why does he get some of that and I don't?" he asks, pouting. His eyes dance, and I lean up on tiptoes to kiss him, light and chaste.

"Because he was lonely and you had the pleasure of my company all afternoon. Now, if you want *any* of that, I suggest you get that ass in gear and pack."

I step away and eye the two men as they move around the room, gathering what little they have sprawled out. My essentials—my computer bag and a small overnight bag—are already waiting by the door. My phone buzzes in my pocket, and I fish it out. Kevin.

Kevin: Call me. Now.

Dread forms in my belly, and I swallow hard. I need to deal with this, even if I don't particularly want to.

"Um, guys? I'm going to head down—get the car brought up. Ok? Ash, remember—"

He waves the hat and sunglasses at me before I can say anything further, and I smirk. "Right. Disguise. Okay, I'll see y'all in a few." I say and slip out before either can push me with questions.

Down the hall, I wait impatiently for the elevator to arrive then breathe a sigh of relief. It's empty. Good.

My fingers shake as I dial the number. Kevin answers on the first ring, his voice a mean growl that makes me cringe. Even here.

135

"Where the fuck are you?"

"Vegas. I believe you knew Knox was planning on getting out of town for a while."

He goes quiet. Then lets out a single sharp bark of laughter. "The bastard told you."

"What the hell were you thinking, giving him an ultimatum like that?" I demand. "Shit like that doesn't work on Asher. All you did was drive him away."

"I was trying to scare him into staying in the city," Kevin snaps. "It's not like you can stay on his account forever. He's the lead in fucking *Black Tides*, Megan."

I stiffen. "What the hell is that supposed to mean?"

"It means I need someone more responsible and experienced taking care of him. He's gotten too big for you."

I laugh. "He's always been too big a name for me, Kevin. That's why you gave me the job—you had to make the talent happy."

"If you won't put out, I don't think you're making him that happy."

"Fuck you," I snap. "I won't whore myself because you want Knox smiling in the morning. And despite not sleeping with him, he is still thriving. I don't know what the hell game you're playing, but taking my client won't actually help him."

There's a moment of silence, and then, "He isn't *your* client, Megan. He never was. He's mine, and I can do whatever

I feel is best for him and his career. And I can fire you, for insubordination."

"Try," I say, my voice soft, almost a purr. "You try to fire me. I'll slap you with a lawsuit so fast your head will spin."

"You would destroy your own reputation, if you came after me. No one would believe you didn't follow orders."

I shift, juggling the phone and my bag as I hand the valet ticket to the driver. He eyes me, and I flash a smile that makes him grin before he turns away.

"Kevin. I don't need people to believe I didn't. The publicity alone will build my name."

"What do you want, Megan?"

"I want my client. I want you to back the fuck off. I'll get him—healthy and sane—to the set in February. And I will put him back in the limelight, before then. But you'll take a step back and let me work. Let me do this my way."

"And if I say no?"

I shrug. "You can't stop it, Kevin. I'm doing this. I couldn't get Ash back to the city right now if I tried—and I won't. I would rather do this without dodging your phone calls and assorted bullshit. It'll be easier that way."

"Will you tell me what you're planning?"

My stomach twists, and I shake my head. "No. I won't. But if getting Asher in the news is what you want, I promise you that I will get him there. In a week or so."

I hesitate, falling quiet as Kevin weighs the options. He'll agree to this—he doesn't have much of a choice.

"Fine. But I want daily updates—a text or an email. If you don't do that, the deal is off."

"Deal," I say shortly. "Expect the first one tomorrow." Without waiting for him to start gloating, I hang up the phone and focus on calming my nerves.

Asher

By some minor miracle, we make it to the car without any incidents. There are a few whispers, but that could simply be the result of two attractive men walking through a hotel together.

I wonder what those whispers would say if they knew we'd shared a woman last night. I smirk, shifting my bag a little. Luca's dark gaze flicks to me, and I shake my head, ignoring the questioning stare. Not the time or place.

"Are you sure this is what you want?" he asks, and I shrug.

"I don't know. I'm honest enough to admit that. But what's the harm in trying?"

He opens his mouth to say something, then shakes his head, his lips compressed into a hard line. He's angry. I slow, frowning at him, and he shakes his head. "What?"

"Nothing. It's not worth it. We'll talk later," he says, striding past me and wrapping an arm around Megan. She glances over her shoulder, her gaze brightening a little when she sees me. I move to where they stand, a few steps away. She gives me a searching stare, and I force a smile as the valet brings our car around. As Megan shoulders her computer bag and Luca leads the way outside, it occurs to me that this will be the best thing to ever happen to me. Or the worse.

I follow them to Luca's Jeep Compass, and he looks at me. "Who's driving?"

Megan eyes the two of us briefly then plucks Luca's keys from his fingers. "I am."

I stare at her for a split second and see the amused mischief dancing in her eyes. She winks and slides into the front seat.

Which leaves the interesting option of who takes the front.

Luca opens the back door, sliding in and across the tan seat with practiced ease. I feel a moment of hesitation and wonder why. He won't molest me in the car, and it's not as if I'm not interested. I shake the thoughts and follow him in.

Megan squeals, a startlingly happy noise. I grin, and she taps the gas, setting us into motion.

Luca relaxes next to me, shifting slightly. His thigh brushes against mine, and I glance over at him. He's got his sunglasses on. I force myself to relax against the seat.

Then we're on the road, and the music fills the car as I absorb Luca's presence and we leave Vegas behind.

Sweet Ruin

Chapter Twelve

Luca

There were reasons why I wanted a road trip. Good reasons—the sheer amount of time we are forced to spend together, and the intimacy of spending so much time in close quarters. And there is the fact that, every night, we will be finding a small hotel room—and all the opportunities that affords.

Many, many reasons.

But after six hours in a car with Megan and Asher, I'm ready to strangle them or fuck them, and neither is showing a damn sign of sexual frustration.

I lick my lips as Meg coasts through a small town in Arizona, just south of Phoenix. It's dark, and I'm hungry and horny. The first moderately impressive hotel I see, I point to.

"There."

"It looks kinda shady," Megan says doubtfully.

I bite back my groan. "We're sleeping, Megan. It doesn't need to be the Hyatt."

She makes a grumpy noise, but heads in that direction. Asher leans into me, his lips brushing my ear. "Is that all we're doing?"

I twist to him, my lips a breath from his. "Not a shot in hell."

He inhales sharply, and I smirk. The car comes to an abrupt halt, and I spill out, fueled by anger and hormones.

"I'll get a room," I say, shutting the door before Asher follows me.

The lobby is quiet, a lonely girl sitting by herself at the front desk. "I need a room. With a king sized bed."

She blinks at the firm tone, but clacks at her keyboard. "ID?"

I fish it and my credit card out, slapping them onto the counter almost hostilely. She gives me a concerned look, but doesn't say anything else as she files the info. I use the quiet and space to get a handle on my temper. By the time she asks for my signature, I feel like I have a thin semblance of control. I flash her an apologetic smile as I scribble my name.

She smiles shyly as I take the key and head back to where Meg and Knox are waiting.

"We're around the back—room 215."

Asher is smiling, an expression I find annoying at the moment. Meggy hums lightly to herself as she steers around the side of the little hotel. "Do you guys want to order something for delivery? I don't want to get back in that car for the next dozen hours, if I can help it."

"Not pizza," Asher says.

"Bad Chinese?" she says, her voice hopeful.

"I will never understand your fascination with bad ethnic food, darling."

She laughs and stops the car. "It's comforting, English. Like an ugly, worn out pair of shoes."

He looks bewildered. "Why not just replace them?"

Megan makes eye contact, a smile lighting her bright green eyes. I shake my head slightly, my mood shifting at the banter.

Meg is wired, a bouncing bundle of energy, as Asher and I grab the bags from the back of the car. Her hair is a greasy mess, her clothes rumpled from travel.

She looks adorable and gorgeous.

"Come on," she says, snatching the key from my hand and scurrying to the door. I follow, eyeing her.

This is more than an excess of energy going on here— she's nervous.

Which we need to nip in the bud.

I step into her as she slides the key into the lock, her lush, jean clad ass cuddled against my obvious erection. She shivers, and I nudge into her with my hips. "Inside, lovely girl."

She doesn't say anything, just shoves the door open.

I toss my bags aside and grab her by the hips, turning us both so she's pressed between me and Asher. His hands come up and catch her by the shoulders, and Megan whimpers as he lowers his head, nibbling at the nape of her neck. "That," he murmurs, "is something I've wanted to do since we left Vegas."

She's staring up at me, her eyes hazy with desire, her nerves a sour aftertaste. It's not enough.

"Asher. She's thinking too much."

His eyes dart up to me, and a thoughtful expression flits across his face.

"Fuck her," he says, that soft accent thickening.

She gasps, her mouth falling open. He leans down, laying a trail of kisses down on her shoulder. "You'd like that, hmm, pet?"

She nods, limply, and my dick twitches. She's almost panting. I want to. So bad, I can taste it. I force myself to step back. "Is that what you want, Megan? Me?"

She licks her lips and shakes her head, slowly. "I want you both."

I let my gaze flick to Asher. He's holding her by the waist, and he smirks at me. "What are you waiting for?"

I move, catching her and pulling her from his arms without any fanfare. He laughs as I back her toward the bed, and I spare him a quick glance. "You're wearing too many clothes."

He pulls his shirt over his head, and I let myself appreciate the view for a few seconds then turn back to Megs. She's watching Asher strip, but I want her attention on me, for the moment. And I want her out of those jeans.

"Don't move," I murmur, dropping to my knees. I unfasten her jeans and peel them down slowly. She's wearing black boy shorts with white trim and a tiny bow. They might be the sexiest thing I've ever seen.

I lean in and kiss her hip bone. She shivers under me, and I feel her sway. I nudge her back until she lies down on the bed. There's a whisper of movement, the creak of bed springs, and I glance up to see Asher stretched alongside her, kissing her as his hand tugs her shirt up.

Without thinking, I kiss the soft inside of her thigh, sucking softly, and she arches against me. I laugh and reach for the hem of her panties.

"I don't think I'll ever get tired of seeing that," Asher says, his voice hoarse.

"She has a pretty pussy, doesn't she?" I say, looking at him. He's staring, his erection twitching, and I smirk. Then I lick her, a soft, flicking touch that has her groaning. Her hands find my head, and she jerks me to her pussy. I lick her again, and she thrusts against my tongue, looking for that little bit of penetration. I move higher, delicately running my tongue over her clit as she whimpers in frustration. Slowly, I ease a two fingers into her and she grinds down on them as I suck on her clit.

The orgasm comes faster than I expect, out of nowhere. Megan whimpers once, and then her body tightens, a sudden contraction of her muscles as the orgasm slams into her. I slide up her body, and Asher catches me, startling me with a kiss. For a second, I don't know what to do—how to respond—and then his teeth nip at my lip. I groan, fisting a hand in his hair as he licks into my mouth. Tiny fingers wrap around my dick, and I break away to look down.

Megan wiggles around a little, and Asher's head drops back, his eyes rolling as she takes him into her mouth. I catch his lips again, taking his groan as she sucks him deep. Then I shift, grabbing a condom and rolling it on before I slide deep into her. She makes a strangled noise, and I shudder at the tight clasp of her pussy on me.

"Tell me," Asher grits out. I groan, struggling to push off my orgasm. As often as I've thought of this, my imagination doesn't compare to the reality of being inside her for the first time.

"Tight. Shit, she's tight."

"Fuck her, Luc," he rasps, thrusting slowly. I do what he says, adjusting her legs and pulling out until she's squirming and whimpering. Then I drive deep into her, and she screams around his dick.

Asher is staring at us, his gaze riveted on where my cock is thrusting into her tight little pussy, and she's whimpering, these hot little noises that are driving me fucking crazy. I can feel the orgasm building, my balls tight and heavy. Asher reaches out and pinches her nipple and Megan shudders.

Our girl likes it a little rough, then. I fuck her harder, a relentless rhythm.

"Fuck, that's good, sweetheart," Asher gasps, and she sucks him deep into her mouth. His eyes go wide, and he makes a choked noise, thrusting into her mouth as he comes.

She's smiling when she pulls back, and Asher laughs, a shaky noise. Her eyes drift to me, and I roll my hips, hitting a spot that makes her gasp.

"Make her come apart," Knox says, and I glance at him. He's cleaned up, his dick half erect. I swallow and thrust harder, dropping down. Meg arches into my weight, and I roll my hips, thrusting faster. She kisses me, and I reach between us, feathering my thumb over her clit as she nips at my lips, her tongue teasing against mine. She shudders, going rigid, her eyes unfocused. My name is a garbled sound that's almost unrecognizable, spilling from her lips as her orgasm slams into her.

I thrust again. Once. Twice. And then my own climax tackles me, and I groan, my eyes closing as the pleasure sweeps over me like a tidal wave. For a long, boneless moment, I ride the wave of pleasure, lost in the erotic haze of Megan.

Asher is still hard, and I feel a moment of guilt as I pull out. Meggy whimpers, a low needy noise, and curls on her side. "Sleepy." She murmurs.

"Do you always get tired after sex?" I tease, and Asher laughs.

She peeks an eye at him and frowns. "Asher."

"I'm fine. You'd be turned on, too, if you watched the two of you together." He leans down, placing a chaste kiss on her lips. I finish cleaning up and tug on a pair of shorts before padding back to the bed and curling up against Megan's back.

"Do you want to shower and eat? Or just sleep?"

Her stomach rumbles, loudly, and Asher laughs. "I guess we have our answer."

"No!" she complains, cuddling into the pillow.

I glance at her and shrug to Asher. "I'm hungry. If gorgeous here wants to sleep, we'll eat without her."

"Bad Chinese?"

I nod, and he grabs the phone, calling the front office for the local delivery. Megan is half dozing on the bed, and I reach down, pulling a blanket over us as Asher orders.

Asher

I hang up and stand, stretching. Luca glances up at me. "She's asleep," he murmurs.

"Is this a normal thing for her?"

"How would I know?" he asks, a smile turning his lips. "I haven't been with her before, English."

I hesitate, and then, "But she was your roommate."

"Megan has never been into sharing—she always assumed I wanted her and Sun. And that's not her thing."

I shift. "So. This"—I gesture at us—"isn't unusual for you?"

He laughs, a startled noise. "No. Sorry, dude."

I flush and look away. For some reason, I'd got it in my head that this was some heavy, new experience. Even though I knew about Sun and his fondness for threesomes—I thought this was special. And it might be—for me. For Megan. But this is normal for Luca.

"How did you get started, in this?"

A shadow slips across his face, there and gone too quickly to pinpoint. "It's a long story."

I cock my head to the side and study him. There is a hint of panic to his handsome features that I haven't seen before, and it worries me. "We have the time, Luc."

He flinches, a tiny movement that catches my attention. I take an emotional step back and nod at Megan. "She says you're close to your roommate—Sun."

A smile, not shadowed, fills his face. "Yeah. She was one of my best friends in high school. We were inseparable. When I decided to come to LA to work, she came with me. I can't imagine the past four years without her."

"And yet, she's not here—and we are. Why?"

"Sun isn't interested in this, long term."

I go still. "Do you think we are?"

He shrugs and rolls onto his back, away from Megan. She shivers. "I don't know. But I want her."

"And me."

He looks at me, his gaze clear and steady in a way it hasn't been all night. "I want to know what makes you tick. I've watched you, Asher. You're talented and a good man, and she adores you—which means something to me. But I also feel like you're running from something, and I don't think you even know what it is."

I stare at him, stunned. No one has ever called me out like that, no one but my mother. Even Megan, who can see through my bullshit better than anyone I know, has never called me on it. Not like this.

"Why are you so miserable?" he asks, his voice a soft whisper. I open my mouth to answer—

And there is a brisk knock on the door. Dinner is here. The tension drains away, and I stand in a rush, opening the door. The delivery man blinks, startled by me, but he doesn't comment other than to thank me for the tip. I nod and kick the door closed. Luca still hasn't moved, lying across the bed by Megan, watching me. I think he's waiting for an answer, and I don't have one for him. I busy myself with the plates, opening little boxes of rice and chicken and noodles. He comes to his feet, moving quietly around the room until he's standing near me. I can feel the heat of his body, but he doesn't push me. Instead, he takes the cardboard container of garlic chicken and pours some onto a plate. The task is so damn domestic, it throws me for a moment.

Sometimes, though, you need the normal and domestic. To keep you grounded.

"It would appear that we both have secrets, huh?"

"They're the spice of life," I shoot back, taking my plate and dropping onto the end of the bed. Luca laughs.

"Nah, man. They really aren't."

"Then why don't you get some off your chest," I challenge.

He shakes his head, a smile on his lips and sadness in his eyes. I don't like it—that sadness. "What do you think of *Black Tides?*"

It's an abrupt change of subject, and I pause, a bite of rice on my fork. Stare at him hard. I had forgotten, somehow, that he would be working with me on the film. "Will this make things awkward on set?" I ask abruptly.

He shrugs, glancing down. "What?"

I set my plate aside, and lean forward, nipping at his ear lobe. Wide eyes dart up to mine and I catch his lips in a quick kiss. It's different from kissing Megan. Luca's lips are fuller, softer, with a rasp of rough dry skin. I lick at his lips, without thinking, and he shifts, his hand fisting in my hair. His tongue strokes along mine, a touch that has my blood racing.

I pull back quickly, and Luca laughs, a low, husky noise. It doesn't help me get my shit under control.

"Nah, man. There shouldn't be any awkwardness at all."

He's grinning, a knowing little smile that I can't decide if I want to smack or if I want to do something to make him do it again. I sit back in my chair and pick at dinner. Glance at the sleeping girl on the bed.

"She's amazing, isn't she?" I say.

Luca shifts, twisting around to look at her. Red hair spills around her, and I want to play with it. Not that playing with a girl's hair while she's sleeping isn't creepy as fuck.

"You knew, right away, that she was special," he says.

I glance over at him, frowning. "She said something— that first day, you flirted. But the second, you were quiet— watching her. It really freaked her out. I figured it out though—especially after she quit and you agreed to play it by her stupid rules. You knew she was special and wanted to keep her."

I swallow hard. How did he see through me so effortlessly? Without even knowing me—because he hadn't, not then. We hadn't even met.

"She is special. You know, she doesn't give a fuck what or who I am. She just bullies me through it."

"I remember the first time you went off the reservation," he says, staring at his plate. "She was so scared— she knew if anything happened to you, it'd come down on her. Kevin had been looking for an excuse to fire her since she started. And he didn't warn her, you know. That you had a tendency to just vanish. So she was frantic, called me and

Sunny to help look for you. We went everywhere. And about twelve hours before you got back, the worry just vanished and she was livid."

"I remember her being angry."

"She wanted to kill you." He laughs. "She didn't care who you were or how big a star—she was furious, and she wanted your head on a fucking platter. I don't know how you managed to walk out of that alive."

I remember when he's talking about—it was after a particularly rough press junket. I'd slipped out without warning her. Spent a few days in a coastal town where no one knew or cared who the hell I was. I was sunburnt and sand blasted, my hand busted from a pickup game of basketball, when I came back. And I was well rested and happy.

She'd been furious, a quiet little mountain ready to explode in my kitchen. "She threatened to quit," I say. "Meggy always could get me to back down, if she did that and I knew she meant it. I would do just about anything to keep her working for me."

He nods, a tiny smile curving his lips. "I know."

Sweet Ruin

Chapter Thirteen

Luca

"So." Megan adjusts her glass and shifts on her side of the booth. We've been on the road for six hours already, and only stopped because English is starving and a whiny little bitch when he's hungry. And if I have to see him eat corn nuts again, I might throw up.

"What?" I say, cautiously, eyeing her. She smiles, a bright chipper expression that is vaguely terrifying.

"What happened with Sun?"

My stomach drops. I'm not ready to talk about this—about why Sun can never be more than she is right now. Megan has believed something for so long, and if I tell her the truth now...

"She got engaged."

Megan pauses, and Asher, in a pair of dark glasses and a ball cap, leans forward. "But Megan said you two were—"

"We're not, okay," I snap. His eyes go wide, and Megan's breath hisses out. "I haven't been with Sun for almost six months."

There's a breath of silence, and the waitress intrudes, dropping off our plates. It's loud and awkward, and she's smacking her gum so loudly I can feel my temper fraying.

"We're fine!" Megan snaps. The girl looks startled, and Asher shoots Meg a quelling look.

"Thanks. We're good," I mutter. The waitress retreats, and Megan frowns at her burger and then looks at me. "What the hell do you mean, you haven't been together for six months? You live with her. You're in love with her—what about that girl from two weeks ago, that y'all fucked in the bathroom?"

I shake my head. "Stranger sex with her is a bad habit—it's not a relationship. Sun wants something I can't give her."

"What?" The question comes from Ash.

I shake my head, hard. "I'm not ready to talk about that. I need you to respect that."

"And I need to know how you could just leave Sun like that!" Megan says shrilly.

"Because I can't!" I snap. "I can't be with her—she wants what we had in the past, and I can't do that. No one can."

They're staring at me, blue and green gazes mixed with concern and anger. And I want to run because I'm not ready for this—I need more time before I tell them, and not over fucking bacon cheeseburgers at a truck stop diner. Not when I'm just getting Asher to trust me and, if I close my eyes, I can still feel Megan coming apart under me.

But you don't get to pick the time and place, do you?

"Sun and I grew up together. I told you that, right?"

Megan nods, and Asher leans across her to snag the salt. "We went to school together, and we were the best of friends. She lived maybe a block away—and we'd constantly be at each other's houses. But the first time I met her, I hated her."

Megan jerks, startled. I give her a wry smile. "She showed up at Dylan's house."

"Who is Dylan?"

How long since I've talked about him? Four years— four years, six months, twenty-two days.

"Dylan Carter. He lived down the street—between Sun and me. His dad worked at the same bank my mother did, and his mom would babysit us during the summer. We got along great—it wasn't one of those situations when you had to hang out with some lame kid. Dylan was amazing. The older we got, the more interested he got in sports, but he was so smart. He studied ancient history like kids today study sports stats. He knew everything about Alexander the Great and the Aztecs. The dude could go on for hours—it drove me absolutely crazy, sometimes. But I mean, he loved it. You don't squash something someone you care about loves." I stare at my food, for a minute, a smile on my lips.

"What about Sun?"

"She showed up the summer before we started sixth grade. She was this over-exuberant personality, all over the place, and Dylan fell for her, hard. She'd settle down, when we were practicing—we both were on the football team, and she loved watching us play. I hated her intrusion, you know? We had this great little world, and she just invaded and wouldn't get the hell out. And then, she just wormed her way into both our hearts. She was so sweet, even when I knew my best friend loved her. I got used to her, I guess. She was there, constantly."

I shrug, glancing up. "You can't pinpoint the moment you fall in love. All I knew is that the day we started freshman year, they were a couple and I was following them around and I just looked up and I knew. I loved her. I had been in love with Dylan for years, so that wasn't a shock—but she was. And I was ok with being in love with them, even if they never found out. Because they had each other, and they were happy."

Megan's eyes are wide and scared—she's never heard this. Our history. Sun and I don't talk about it. Ever.

"Freshman year we dominated on the field, and Sun bounced around the sidelines and tried to get me to hook up with the other cheerleaders. But she'd always sabotage it. She'd drive the girls off as fast as she could get them to agree to date me. Dylan was just as bad. Girls knew he was my best friend. They'd ask him about me, and he'd blow them off. They were in love and happy together, and I was alone and happy for them, but miserable. I was lonely. And they knew it. So one night, we got into this huge fight. It was after another disastrous date. A cheerleader from our rival had made a pass at me at a party, and I set up a double. Sun was furious." I laugh, a little.

"She alternated between flirting with me and being the biggest bitch imaginable to my date, until Clarice finally just walked out. I always wonder what she thought about us—and how fucking dysfunctional we were.

"Anyway, as soon as she was gone, Sun cheered up, went back to her friendly self while she made out with Dylan. And I lost it, you know? I just couldn't get it. We left and ended up screaming at each other in the school parking lot."

I go quiet, remembering.

"*You can't keep doing this! You're not with me. You can't be jealous.*"

"*They don't deserve you.*" *From her. And Dylan, watching. A strange look in his eyes, a look I'd recognize the rest of my life. The screamed declaration and the kiss that he did nothing to stop. His quiet movement around us as I made out with his girlfriend. His soft orders as we stripped on the football field and she sucked me off, as I slid into her*—I shake my head.

"I think they knew, for a long time, that we'd be more—it was not so much an *if* as a *when*. And after that first night, it was different. We weren't open about it, but I quietly took myself off the market. The dates with other couples at school stopped. We spent more time in." I sigh, shaking my head fondly.

"It was a good time for us. We ran that school, you know. Some people suspected—there would be rumors that she was cheating, or with both of us—but as long as Dylan and I kept the team winning, no one gave shit. We thought it would never end."

We were fucking idiots. Blissfully happy and stupid enough to think it would never end.

No one gets that. No one gets to keep their slice of heaven forever.

"Dylan was killed Christmas of our senior year. We'd just gotten accepted at UGA, and we were headed there in the fall—all of us. We were so unbelievably happy. The kind of happy that doesn't end, you know?" I can't look up. I can't face the shock and pity in their eyes—it's why I left home.

"He was driving home—he and Sun had driven out to my grandparents' farmhouse, and he had to go back to the city. We tried to talk him into staying—it was snowing and the roads were iced over. But he had to take his baby sister shopping the next morning, and he wanted to give me and Sun some time alone—it was his way of saying Merry Christmas. So he left, and we let him. And the next day, he was dead—they found his car wrapped around a tree. He'd been pinned in the seat and bled out." For a moment, I'm swimming in it again, the searing heartbreak and crushing grief. It doesn't go away. How could it—he was my best friend and lover. How do you get over losing that?

You don't.

"Luca," Megan whispers, her tone rich and raspy with shock. Pity?

"After that, I couldn't be alone with Sun. I tried, but every time, all I could think about was Dylan slowly dying while I fucked our girlfriend. And I couldn't get over that. She moved here with me because it was as far as we could go to get away from the memories. But she wants to recreate what we had."

"And you don't?" Asher says, his voice cautious. Like I might hit him and he'd like to avoid that.

"I love Sun. I loved them both and always will. But no one can replace Dylan, and I can't have with her what we had together. It was never going to work, just the two of us. Dylan held us together and made us better. She's trying to replace that and..." I shake my head, helplessly. "I can't do it. I don't want it. I don't want to look at her and see him—and I do."

Megan exchanges a quick glance with Asher, and I can almost hear what they're thinking. Gently, she says, "Sweetie? Is that any different from us?"

I shrug. "There isn't an us. We're fooling around and its fun—but we aren't a life-changing thing, Meg. Not unless you both want it to be."

I hold my breath, watching the shock stutter across her face, and Asher's wide eyes. *Bad idea.* I flash a smile and shove away from the table, stalking out of the little diner and into the bright afternoon sunlight. "Luca!" I hear Megan calling me, but I don't stop.

I don't talk about Dylan. In the four years since he died, I've avoided talking about him—it helped that we left town after his death, after I dropped out. No one complained—the football season was over.

My lips twist, a little bit of loathing for the town we came from and a little bit of disgust with myself.

I slide down the side of the building, slip my sunglasses on, and let the memories wash over me. Distantly, I'm aware of Megan sitting next to me, and I tense worriedly as she gets comfortable.

But she doesn't talk—just tilts her head back and lets the sunlight warm her skin.

"I'm sorry, Luc. That you lost your friend that way. I—there's nothing to say. Just I'm sorry."

That simple. That useless phrase applied with a little bit of conviction.

"Why don't you ever talk about him?"

"I didn't want to share him, at first. But then it just became easier, and no one knew him. I wanted to be happy—and I'm not, not really. But I got better at pretending, until it got to be so damn good, I couldn't tell if I was actually that happy and charming, or if I showed the world that because they expected it and made my life easier."

Megan shifts, resting her head against my arm. "And with me?"

"You, lovely girl, was because I didn't want to see the look I see in your eyes now. Cautious pity. I can't take that from you—it would break my heart."

She looks surprised, and I start to look away. Small fingers catch me, and I go still as they caress at my jaw, a soft pressure turning me to face her. I stare at her, and she smiles, a soft expression, before leaning forward and brushing her lips over mine lightly. Once. Twice. The third time, I groan and she huffs a laugh. I growl and catch her by the nape of her neck, drag her closer, kissing her for real. Until all thought of the past and Dylan and laughter and loss are gone, and she's panting in my arms, her little hands twisting in my shirt. I nip at her lip once more, and she arches into me, her eyes closed as she revels in the sensations. I grin and slap the curve of her ass, where my hand has somehow drifted.

"Come on, lovely girl. Let's see if we scared English off."

Asher

I expected something. There is too much hanging on Luca for the model to not have something heavy in his past. But this— his best friend and lover, dying while he was with the woman they loved.

I had asked how he got started in triads. I didn't expect this, though. Not that it was his first experience, was as natural to them as breathing. I didn't expect him to tell me he started doing it in high school and can't imagine life without it.

I watch as Megan hurries across the parking lot, chasing Luca down.

He doesn't want Sun. But what does he want? And can I be that? I'm honest enough to acknowledge that I want him—that I had wanted him before this story. Sleeping with him seems less a distant possibility and closer to a reality.

I lick my lips and pay the waitress, standing to leave. The diner is close to empty, but there is one table of teen girls, and they're staring at me a little too intently.

Fuck.

I tug my cap a little lower and adjust my sunglasses. Except, I don't have any. Luca broke them this morning when we stopped for gas, and I haven't had a chance to replace them. Need to fix that shit—immediately.

I look out the window for Megan and directly into a camera. Fuck a duck. I mutter a curse and head for the door. The teen girls are already up and moving, and I know I'm not getting out of here without dealing with them.

But a group of five teen girls never stays at five teen girls. They spawn—they've already called friends and told them I'm here, and it's going to get out of hand quick.

I text Meg a quick SOS and paste a smile on my face.

"You're Isaac Kreigh, aren't you?" one of the girls asks, her voice squeaky and excited.

Her friend rolls her eyes. "Isaac is a character—*his* name is Asher." She shakes her head, smiling at me like I'll understand, and all I want is for her to vanish, quickly. With her friends.

"I'm sorry, ladies, I'm afraid," I start.

"Then you are Knox. Asher Knox of Kreigh fame?"

"I'm really not doing a public appearance," I force out.

"Can we just get a picture?" the quiet girl says shyly, and it breaks my defense. The shy ones are my fucking kryptonite. I close my eyes and count to ten, and then flash the slightly crooked smile that won me the Isaac Kreigh role.

The girls squeal and shift, plastering themselves to me. In my pocket, I feel my phone vibrate, but the bubbly girl's ass is too close to my thigh—she's practically rubbing against me—and I can't reach it without groping her. I'm not that desperate to get away.

"Smile!" she chirps, and they snap a quick shot, before giggling and rearranging themselves. I try not to fidget as they argue about poses, eventually handing off the camera to the shy girl to take better shots as they pose around me.

After five minutes—five long fucking minutes—my phone buzzes again, and this time I am desperate. I dislodge bubbly—Mindy—and hold up a finger.

"Where the hell are you, English?"

"Get the car and get over here—just follow the teen girls," I mutter.

"Shit," he hisses, and the call ends.

"Are you going to sign my bag?" Mindy pouts. She's nibbling her lip, trying hard for seductive—and failing miserably.

I grab the bag—it's a big gaudy thing, a fake Chanel. For a spiteful second, I want to tell her preening friends, but that would be cruel, and it's not me they want—it's Isaac. I just have the character's face. I swallow and scribble my signature, adding the loopy signature I perfected for Isaac. She smirks and goes on tiptoes to kiss my cheek, a gesture I am barely able to keep from recoiling from. When her hand slips into my pocket, though, I do flinch, taking a sharp step backward. She giggles, and turns to show her friends—including the three more who just arrived, their eyes wide and disbelieving.

The car pulls up behind me, and I let out a sigh of relief. "I'm sorry, ladies. I've got to be on my way, though—my agent is going to kick my ass for putting us behind."

One of them launches herself at me—I see it before she even moves, the intention and the way she gathers herself just before she comes at me. I catch her out of reflex, and her lips are mashed down against mine, coarse and demanding, her tongue stabbing at my mouth with a disgusting lack of finesse or skill.

I shudder and drop her without fanfare. My civility drops away, and I spin to the car, shoving a bright eyed redhead aside as I pull the door open wide enough to slip in. Megan taps the gas, hard enough that the engine revs, and the girls dart back.

She hits the gas as she shoves the Compass into drive, and we lurch forward in a burst of speed.

"Fuck," I snarl, wiping a hand over my mouth. From the backseat—shit, I got in the front—Luca touches my shoulder. I flinch. "Don't fucking touch me," I snap. Megan's eyes dart over to me, but I'm ignoring her.

I hate it. I hate the grabbing hands and the eager smiles and the shit shoved on me—which reminds me. I delve into my pocket.

It's a pair of silk panties, bright pink. Obviously worn. In the backseat, Luca chokes, and I want to scream, anything to get this disgusting shitty feeling out of my head. Without comment, Megan hits the window button. It eases down, and I toss the dirty panties and the number she also shoved into my pocket.

It helps a little, to ease the gross, panicked feeling I'm fighting.

Luca opens his mouth in the back seat, and Megan shakes her head. She reaches into her purse, without looking away from the road, and hands me an iPod, the earbuds wrapped around it. Then a novel. I tuck the earbuds in and curl up against the window as the music blasts through my ears, drowning out thought and the people who demand so much of me, the way I feel so fucking cheap and gross. Everything. And when the knot of anxiety loosens its choke hold, when I can see past the anger and start to think, I open the book and let the words obliterate that too.

Chapter Fourteen

Megan

I can feel Luca's agitation in the backseat, but I'm not talking until I know Asher is past the worst of it. Which, truthfully, could take hours. Sometimes, after a really busy press junket, he's a mess for days. It's hard to tell, but I do know that contact won't be welcome until he's through this—anything could set him off.

I choke on my sigh. As much as I adore Knox, the drama of dealing with him and his inevitable mood swings is exhausting. But this one was my fault. I knew people were watching us, after Luca left the table so abruptly, and I knew that, left alone, Asher would be scrutinized and eventually someone would put things together.

It's hard to be the face of one of the most successful franchises in recent history and *not* attract attention.

It was the role that made Asher—it propelled him from Shakespeare in dingy London theatres to the limelight of Hollywood. *Far and Gone* was a cult phenomenon that grew with each season of the show, until Isaac Kreigh and Asher Knox were household names—and almost interchangeable. When the series ended, fans were furious. They wanted more

Isaac. Wanted to know what happened to their favorite time-traveling boy next door.

Which is why the movie coming out in July is such a big deal. It's the last time fans get to see Isaac and follow him through time.

For Asher—and me—the premiere and ensuing madness can't be over fast enough. The sooner it's over, the sooner he can move on to anything but Isaac.

Like *Black Tides*. I catch my lip between my teeth and try to focus on that, and not how things could go wrong taking the two men who are beginning to matter so much to me back home.

It's not that I don't love Branton—I do. It was the perfect town to grow up in, an idyllic hideaway. But it's where I grew up—and everyone in the city knew who I was. Everyone knew David Beauchamp and his oldest daughter, and me—the little girl he'd taken in.

Some people—ok, a lot of people—had been confused when I left for LA. Why be a little fish in a big pond when I could be a Beauchamp in Branton?

But staying home meant two things—working for Daddy and living in Nik's shadow. Neither was something I was particularly comfortable with. I'd rather be the little fish than Nik's baby sister.

I blink hard, trying to force my worry aside—I'm not even sure Nik will be home. After the divorce, she might have cut and run—she always talked about leaving Branton.

Of course, Nik talked about a lot of things.

Late that night, we stop at a tiny Holiday Inn. I'm exhausted from driving and the stress of an unraveling Asher sitting next to me. And Luca, with his watching eyes. He touches my arm as Ash stumbles into the bathroom. "What do you need?"

"Vodka. And food? He should eat. We all should." Belatedly, I realize how amazingly wonderful Luca has been, giving us time and silence. I step into him, wrapping my arms around his waist. His come around my shoulders, squeezing me to him, and his lips brush my hair. "Thank you," I say, sleepily. "I know you didn't sign on for the crazy."

His fingers tilt my head up, until I'm staring at his too serious eyes. "I signed up for whatever comes. I knew this was part of the package. Do what you do, lovely—talk him down. I'll be back." He hesitates, then rubs a thumb over the curve of my cheek. "What about you? You doing ok?"

I blink hard and force a wobbly smile. His gentle tone is undoing me, something Luca has always been damn good at. "Fine," I chirp. "I'm fine."

"You're not. But you can tell me after you deal with Ash."

I nod, and he leans down, pressing a quick kiss to my lips before he backs out of the hotel room.

I wait until I hear the Compass back away. Then I take a deep breath and walk to the bathroom. The shower is running, and I'm not sure if it's because he's trying to wash off the afternoon, or if he's falling apart and using the water to mask it. I tap on the door hesitantly then push it open. "Ash?"

He's sitting in the tub, arms looped around his long legs, water pounding down on his head. When he looks up at me, long hair hanging in his startling eyes, I'm left breathless by the desolation in his gaze. I step into the little room and walk over to the tub, ignoring the water splashing me as I crouch next to him.

"Talk to me," I say softly.

"They don't want this," he murmurs, a manic gleam in his eyes. "They want Kreigh, and they want me, because that's what they see—but if the whole world saw me like this, they'd never want me again."

I shrug. "Maybe not. But you'd miss the spotlight."

He barks a laugh. "I'd be able to eat my lunch with a mate in public. Snog my girlfriend without being watched. I don't want *this*, Meggy."

I catch him by the jaw and force his gaze up until he's staring at me. His lips are compressed, an angry line, and I struggle to keep the bite out of my tone. "They are the price, Asher. You have the entire world in love with you—"

"No!" he shouts, jerking away. "They love Isaac. No one sees *me*!"

"I do!" I shout back. His eyes go wide, and I soften my tone, leaning into his space, ignoring the water beating down on us. "I see you. We both see you."

"I'm losing myself, Meg. I'm so scared I'll get swallowed up in the crazy surrounding Isaac, and I don't know how to separate myself from it."

It's a whispered confession, almost drowned out by the sound of the water. "You keep your eyes on us."

His eyes, wide and scared, find mine, almost desperately. "What about when Kevin takes you away? This can't last."

I laugh, softly, and shake my head. "Do you really think I'll let him? You're mine, Ash. I'm not going anywhere." I stand and strip out of my wet t-shirt, peel off my soaked jeans. Good thing we're arriving tomorrow—I'm running out of clean clothes and cute underwear. "Luca will be back soon."

His eyes are a little less panicked, brighter with desire than fear—but he won't follow me out to the bedroom. He's not ready for that, and I know it. So I leave him to the shower and go slip into an oversized t-shirt, sitting on the bed and texting Kevin while I wait for the boys to come to me.

Sweet Ruin

Chapter Fifteen

Luca

Megan has been a twitchy mess all day. She's been quiet and didn't even curse when her phone died—I'm pretty sure that's a first for her. She drums her fingers on the side of the door, and I finally reach across the backseat, catching her hand and stilling her.

She shoots me a look, half apologetic, half annoyed. In the front seat, Asher is oblivious—as he has been most of the day. I'd come back from my food run to find her in a t-shirt and wet hair, Asher lost in a book. Neither had been in the mood for sex or talking, and I hadn't pushed. Instead, we'd eaten and Meg proposed a drinking game while we watched an old Law and Order, and we fell asleep drunk, with Asher cuddled between the two of us.

It felt right.

But that had been hours ago, and the two of them are still wound tight. I squeeze her hand and ask, softly, "What's wrong?"

She flashes me a funny look. "Do you think you can go home again?"

Ah. So that's what this is. A little relief fills me that she isn't freaking out over us.

"No. Not really."

She looks at me, startled, and I shrug. "People change, Megan. They leave home and grow up and change. And when they go back, nothing is the same and everything is, and you can't go back in time."

"But you are going back, aren't you." It's a statement, from Asher.

"Do you really think I've fought this hard for us, only to walk away as soon as I've got it?" I ask, amused. "No, English. I'm not going anywhere."

He meets my gaze in the rearview mirror, a smile ticking his lips up, and I want to kiss him. Right now. Fuck this stupid drive. "How much longer?" I ask, my voice hoarse.

"Soon," she whispers.

I look back at her and shake her shoulders lightly. "Tell us."

"I left this place to find a place that was mine. I grew up in Nik's shadow, expecting to take over for Daddy when he retired from his insurance firm. I love Branton—I went to school here, and I was raised here. But I needed to prove I could be more than this tiny town and Nik's baby sister."

"So you chose the biggest stage in the world to try and make it?"

"Stupid right?" she says, a little bitter.

There's a heartbeat of silence, and then, "Megan, you have—you proven yourself."

She smacks my chest, hard. "No I haven't."

"You're in a car with Asher Knox, a man who threatened to leave his agency for you. And me—I'm a working actor who just landed the lead across from Knox. If that's not making it in Hollywood, what is?"

"I didn't do that—Kevin only gave me the job because I'm Ash's type."

"But that's not why you kept the job. Fuck, if that's all I wanted, you'd have been sent packing months ago, pet. You haven't slept with me—even now that we've fooled around, we haven't shagged. I'm not pissed because he's threatening to take my fuck buddy—I'm pissed because you're the best handler I've had in my career."

She bites her lip, and the calm voice of the GPS tells Asher to take the next exit. His gaze darts to her, and then he eases into the exit lane. She shakes her head as we speed toward the place she comes from, and I find myself torn between wanting to pass it and wanting to see what makes her *her*.

"The problem is, no one will care," she says quietly. "To them, I'll always be Meggy Beauchamp, Nikki's baby sister."

I squeeze her tight to my side, and she shivers as we curve away from the highway, into a tiny town.

It's every little town in America, a picturesque main street still brightened by Christmas lights and charming old-fashioned street lamps. There's a café and deli that look deserted, and to the right, the university sprawls, classic architecture lending to the air of academia. Students scurry through the large swaths of dead grass, braced against the chill. We pass another café, this one much busier, and Megan bounces out of my arms. "Stop!"

For the first time today, her eyes are bright. "We have to go in."

"Where, Meggy?"

She points at the café. Hill of Beans. I eye it and shrug. What the hell, she's finally happy—I'm not going to squash that.

Megan is practically bouncing in place as Asher parks, and we clamber out. The air is cool and crisp and carries the heavy scent of coffee and pastries. Megan abandons us as she hurries to the café and pulls the door open with a clatter.

A slim man, a bit older than us, is standing behind the counter, prepping a drink for the girl standing at the end of the bar. People are scattered around, studying and talking softly, creating a soft ambiance that is instantly soothing.

"Megan Beauchamp." A slow drawl, heavy with southern warmth. Asher steps in behind me, and I look to the speaker. Megan is grinning from ear to ear and squeals as the man comes from behind the counter and wraps her in a rough hug. "You look amazing, darlin'."

"My god, Jeff! This place is gorgeous. Last time I was home you were still in that little cart on campus."

He grins. "We expanded." His gaze flits to me and Asher, briefly, and she steps back, suddenly self-conscious.

"These are some friends—they're in town on research. Knox, and Luca."

Jeff nods amiably, his expression admirably blank. "Jeff Curtis. Good to meet y'all."

"You too."

"Jeff gave me my first job," Megan says, her eyes dancing. "For free, of course."

He smirks and moves back behind the counter. I relax as he puts some distance between himself and Megan, a jealous knot uncoiling.

When did I get jealous?

"How long are you in town?" he asks.

"Not sure. Maybe a few days—maybe a couple weeks. Depends on how long the boys need," she says.

His eyes narrow a little, and then the expression clears. "What can I get you?"

"Any blackberry scones?" she asks hopefully.

He grins and nods. Megan squeals. "Three, a mocha latte, dirty chai, and hot tea."

She reaches for her wallet, and Jeff waves her off, chatting about people and places I've never heard of while he makes our drinks. He scribbles something on the side of

Megan's cup and taps it as he slides the order across the counter.

"Call me. We'll do dinner." She nods and leans across the wooden counter to kiss his cheek. Jeff's gaze softens a little, and then she's pulling away.

"It was good to meet y'all," he calls as we follow Megan out of the little café. I shoot a glare over my shoulder and catch his gaze—he's smiling, a knowing glint to his eyes that pisses me off.

Back in the car, Megan is looser, comfortable and relaxed against her seat. She hums softly, and I don't want to kill that—

"Who the fuck is that?" Asher spits.

Alright, then. We're going to wreck that. Megan jerks, as if slapped. Her eyes, wide and shocked, dart to the backseat, where Asher and I are. He's glaring, and I'm trying to look out the window, but struggling to keep the anger off my face.

"Jeff? We grew up together—he lived a few streets away and used to sit with me when Nik disappeared with Atticus."

"He was a bit friendly for a babysitter, don't you think?"

"I think your being an ass," she snaps. Her gaze darts to me. I meet it and shrug. She huffs a laugh and turns away. "Un-fucking-believable."

We're all quiet as she drives the rest of the way to the hotel. She jerks the car to a stop in the parking lot and explodes from the front seat. Fury makes her entire body stiff—I've seen her like this.

Megan wears her anger like armor, and fuck the people who get in her way when she's on a tear.

"Megan!" Knox shouts, and I grab his arm as she storms inside.

"Don't. Let her have a minute."

"That guy was all over her."

"She has friends, Ash. She had a whole life here, before she left town." He falters, and I shake my head. In the face of his anger and hers, it's easier to let go of my own. Easier to bridge a peace between them.

Which is weird as fuck, because that was always Dylan, before.

"You have to realize we're going to see people here, people we don't know—she had a history, an entire life here before she left. We can't be jealous every time some guy looks at her."

He smirks, slides a glance at me. "You are the only guy who can look at her without me being jealous."

My breath catches, and he shoves the door open, stepping out into the crisp southern air. I watch for a second as he walks toward the elegant hotel, and then he turns and beckons, and I know that I shouldn't go—booking a hotel room with two men is a sure way to kill Megan's reputation in this tiny town. But a smile is playing on his lips and anger is brewing in his eyes, and I wouldn't turn away from them for the world.

Asher

The problem is I'm angry. I'm completely pissed, and I know it, but I can't seem to turn it off. I saw that asshat, the way he hugged Meg. The way his eyes had slid, too appreciatively, over Luca. The flare of recognition tamped down in his eyes when he looked at me.

All of it added up to grate at my nerves and piss me the fuck off, and I want to feel something—something besides dirty and mad.

Megan is smiling and taking the keys from a bright-eyed teen boy, but I know that expression. As soon as she turns away, her smile falls and she scowls. "You and Luca are upstairs—third floor. I'm on the second."

There is a hitch in Luca's step. She doesn't bother slowing to explain, just leads the way to the bank of elevators. I exchange a quick look with Luca, and he frowns. The elevator dings, and I step on first. Megan steps in and skirts to the side, but I catch her by the hips and settle her against me as Luca prowls into the tiny box. The doors glide shut, and he steps into her space, pressing her between us. She whimpers, going soft in my grip, her body loosing that troublesome stiffness.

"Why are you angry?" he murmurs, nipping at her earlobe. I dip down, kissing her neck, and her head falls back to rest on my shoulder.

"You're jealous."

"Yes," I say, softly, and bite down on her neck. She shudders, a full body ripple. My dick hardens. Our girl likes a touch of pain in her sex. "Jeff is a little too friendly."

My hands drift down, away from her hips. I palm Luca's erection, and he hisses, thrusting into the touch. I smile and add, "I won't share. Not either of you. Remember that."

The elevator doors open, and we spill out into the empty hall. She looks sexy as fuck, hair disheveled, nipples hard, and her gaze sleepy. Luca shifts the bag to cover his erection, and I smoother a laugh.

"Why separate rooms?" Luca asks, curiously, as she unlocks the door to her room.

"Appearances," she says. "It's a small town, boys. I need y'all to understand that."

I nod, and she sways over to me, her hips a sexy rhythm I want to memorize.

"When did you know Jeff was gay?"

Luca curses softly at my side, and I shrug. "When he checked Luca out."

She laughs and turns away.

Sweet Ruin

Chapter Sixteen

Megan

"So I'm going to call Atticus, see if we can meet with him tomorrow."

It's late, and we're all sitting on my king-sized bed. The boys retreated to their room when we arrived, showering and settling in, but I wasn't surprised when they came knocking. They were freshly showered and shaved, smelling of soap and minty toothpaste, and I wanted to spend the evening rolling around my bed, but that needed to be tabled until we got in touch with Atticus.

Asher's stomach growls, and I smirk. "And then we can go to Smoky Q and grab some sandwiches."

"Do we have to leave?" Luca murmurs, running a hand over the inside of my thigh. I'm wearing tiny sleep shorts, the first thing I found to put on, and I shiver as he caresses me.

"Yes," Asher says firmly. "Because I'm starving. Now quit groping her and let her do her thing."

Luca sits up, pouting, and Asher leans across me, catching him by the back of his neck and dragging him into a kiss. I stare, my mouth dry as they kiss, and Luca's hand comes up to tangle in Knox's hair. He groans, a low noise that has me squirming on the bed.

When Asher finally pulls away, Luca's breathing is ragged, his eyes dilated with hunger and need. "What was that for?" he asks, his voice tight.

Asher smirks and sits back. "Make your call, pet. I want you two naked. Soon."

Well. When he puts it that way.

I clear my throat and grab my phone, pulling up Atti's number and waiting as it rings through.

"Hello?"

The voice is laughing and feminine, and it isn't my sister, which is so *wrong* it's hard to wrap my head around. I pull the phone away and look at the display. Yep. Right number.

He said he was with someone, but I didn't expect to get smacked in the face with her.

"Megan?" the voice says, my name a puzzled question.

I clear my throat again. "Sorry. Um. I'm trying to reach Atti?"

"He's burning dinner," she says, giggling, and I hear a low masculine voice I recognize. "One second."

There is a bewildering splash of laughter and muffled voices, and then, "Megs?" I relax a little as Atticus' voice smoothes over the line, warming me.

"Hey, Atti. How are you?"

"If my fiancée would leave me alone and let me cook, I'd be better," he growls

"You're *engaged?*"

He hesitates, and then, "Yeah. We got engaged a couple nights ago. I…well, can I talk about it when you get to town?"

"You don't owe me an explanation," I say automatically. He doesn't. After Nik's behavior, I didn't blame him too much for walking away. I just—things change, when you leave home for a year and a half. Even the things that you think will always be the same.

"I'm here," I say into the awkward silence. "We got to town a few hours ago."

"Do you want to meet for lunch tomorrow? I have to go to the big house."

"Sure. You don't mind meeting with my clients?"

"No, of course not. You know I love talking about Jean."

I laugh, remembering the glazed looks Nik and I often had when Atticus would come for dinner and go on a history tangent.

"What time should we be there?"

We make plans to meet at one thirty, and I hang up, dropping my phone onto the bed. Luca is propped up, flipping through the script of *Black Tides.* He looks up as I hang up and smirks up at me. "Dinner?"

I look down, at my state of undress, and nod. "Clothes first."

We spend an hour at Smokey Pig, laughing over chipped sandwiches and fried corn on the cob—a delicacy the boys have never experienced before. A few people do a double take upon seeing us, but it's a relaxed sort of thing—the reaction to the prodigal daughter returning home rather than to her sitting at a table with Isaac Kreigh and a man whose abs have worldwide fame.

It's disconcerting, and strangely nice, to be the one getting attention. I am used to standing in Asher's shadow. Maybe it's comfortable there, because I spent so much time in Nik's shadow.

"I don't understand why you have to fry it, though," Asher says. "It's a perfectly good ear of corn, before you fry it."

"They fry everything, man. They fry Snickers and balls of mayo," Luca interjects, a laugh in his voice.

"Both of y'all shut up. Or I won't share my fried apple pie."

They stare at me like I've lost my mind, and I stick my tongue out then stand and strut to the door. I glance back, once, a smile tickling the corners of my lips. "Y'all coming?"

Both scramble to follow me.

Asher

I've never seen this side of her. She's all laughter and light, and hasn't looked at her phone since we left the hotel.

I'm pretty sure that's some kind of record.

She tosses Luca the keys, and we slip into the back, where she promptly snuggles into my arms with a happy little sigh. I wrap my arms around her, pulling her into my lap, and Luca glances back at us. He hits the blinker and turns onto a side road.

"This isn't the way back," Meg protests.

Luca ignores her and glances back at me. "If she falls asleep because you get her off in the car, I'll kick your ass."

I smirk, and his eyes twinkle with suppressed laughter. Then he turns around and drives, taking random turns. After the second, I lose track—because Megan is soft and warm in my arms and I can't think of anything but how she looked on that cheap hotel bed, lost in pleasure. Without letting myself think of anything else, I kiss her, and she arches into the touch, craning back for my kiss as I stroke a hand down her hip and back up, until her breast is filling my hand and I want these damn clothes off. I shove her shirt up and her bra down, thankful Luca was smart enough to invest in tinted windows when he bought this car. She's panting, her ass pushing against my dick. I break the kiss, groaning as she wiggles against me.

"Fuck, I want you," I hiss, and she laughs, a smoky sound that turns into a whimper when I pinch her nipple between my fingers, tugging just enough to get her attention. She shivers, and I grin, licking at the curve of her neck.

Luca is driving slowly now, his gaze darting to the rearview mirror so often it's a wonder we haven't crashed.

"Should I let you come, pet? Or should I wait and let Luca watch while I fuck you?"

She gasps, and I laugh, sliding a hand down to the button of her pants. I hesitate for a heartbeat, and she shifts impatiently. I pop the button and slip my hand into her jeans, under the silk of her little panties. I groan as I slip a finger through the wet heat pooling between her legs and thrust two fingers into her, the tiniest bit. She whimpers, her hips undulating, and if she doesn't stop that, I'm going to embarrass myself. She twists her head as she moves, shamelessly riding my fingers as she catches my lips in a kiss, her tongue pumping into my mouth. Her hips move faster, a desperate race to her peak, and I reach up with my free hand, rolling her nipple between my fingers. She stiffens, and I feel her body shudder, her pussy tightening around my fingers. Megan whimpers against my lips, a needy, almost broken noise, and I smile as she goes limp.

"Dammit, English," Luca says, his tone tight with irritation and desire. I slip my fingers from her and let her shift to the seat.

Without thinking through my actions, I lean forward and bring my fingers to Luca's lips. I can feel Megan watching us and the wary caution in Luca. But then his lips close over my fingers, and my cock jerks. I wait, barely breathing, as he sucks my fingers clean. Then I sit back and Megan curls into my side, her finger brushing my erection.

"Not now," I say hoarsely. "Wait till we get to the hotel."

Megan

I keep thinking I'll get used to this, being caught between Luca and Asher, both their attention like a hot brand, marking me as theirs.

But then, I thought I could play this off as meaningless sex that would be forgotten once the sheets cooled.

It's so much more than that, and I can't deny it, not anymore. Luca holds my hand as we walk through the hotel, and I wonder, if I kiss him, will he taste like me?

I shake the thought, focusing on the feel of his fingers wound around my own. Asher opens the door to my room as we approach, and I hesitate at the blatant desire in his eyes. His gaze flares, taking us in, and he points. "Sit in the chair, Megan."

Luca

She doesn't protest, dropping my hand and walking across the room to the single chair.

"Undress first," he adds, without looking away from me. Behind him, I see her hesitate, and I wonder if it's from the way he's giving orders, or if it's the order itself. But she reaches for the hem of her shirt, pulling it up and over her head without fanfare. Her hair is a little messed when she drops the top, and then she unsnaps her jeans and peels them down, standing in her heels, bra, and panties.

Asher snaps his fingers lightly, and my gaze darts to him. "What do you want, Luc?" he asks, his voice a soft whisper that sets my blood on fire. It's a challenge, and I catch his fingers, squeezing them.

"I want more than this."

His eyes dilate, and he smirks. "I think Megan needs to see just what she's getting herself into."

I nod and strip out of my shirt. Asher opens his arms, and I step into his space, unbuttoning his shirt with nimble fingers then leaning down, catching the flat disk of his nipple with my teeth. He hisses, a sound so mixed with desire the pain is washed away. Without waiting for his cue, I hit my knees, palming his erection through his jeans. His hips roll into my touch, almost without his permission, and his head falls back. I loosen his belt quickly and shove the jeans and his boxers aside, suddenly desperate to have him.

She whimpers, a sound that twists with his groan, as I take him deep, until the broad head of his cock pushes against the back of my throat. I bob quickly, tightening the suction of my lips and giving him the best fucking blow job I've ever given.

It counts. This counts. More than any relationship I've had since Dylan, this matters. And I'm terrified I'll fuck it up somehow.

Asher's hand is on my head, fingers brushing over the stubble on my scalp, his groans a steady beat in my ears, as I suck his cock.

"She likes this," Asher gasps out, and I fist the base of his dick, giving him a slow stroke. "Shit," he hisses, and I look up to see his eyes have slipped closed.

I smirk. "You're thinking too much, English." I glance over at Megan, who is watching with wide eyes, a flush in her cheeks.

"Come here," I murmur.

She's across the room before the words are out, her breasts pressed against me as I kiss her. There is no finesse in the kiss—it's all raw hunger and teeth and lips that don't line up, and her breathless gasp stealing all rational thought. I nudge her back until she collides with Asher. He sits on the bed, scooting back, and I nod. "Straddle him, sweetheart. Let him have you."

Her eyes go wide, and she flinches as his fingers graze the crease of her ass. "I'm not—"

"You aren't ready for that. But I want to kiss you while he fucks you. So you'll do this."

She takes a deep breath.

Asher

It's awkward as hell—and she looks nervous through the haze of desire. I sit up, leaving nibbling kisses on her spine as I tug her hips so she's hovering over me. Strong hands wrap around my dick, and I thrust into the grip without thought. Luca laughs, and then I can't hear that, can't hear anything, nothing but Megan's soft whimper, and the silky heat of her wrapping around me. I drop back on the bed, my hands holding her hips too hard, and try not to move as she slides down, until I'm buried balls deep in her.

I want to shout in triumph. I want to thrust into her until we're both screaming. I want to see the look on Luca's face. I shove all of that aside and squeeze her hips. "Move, Meggy," I say harshly. "Ride me, love."

It takes a few minutes, a few agonizing slips along my cock, before she finds the rhythm she wants, a shallow rise and fall, her hips working in tiny circles that has me riding the edge. She's gasping, these sexy little noises that are driving me fucking crazy, and falls forward, still working her hips, still chasing that edge.

Luca catches her, kissing her and holding her up as I fuck her. His fingers play over her clit, and she moans, a long drawn out noise that is almost a sob. I shift, my fingers brushing over the curve of her ass, and she tenses a little.

"Relax, love," Luca murmurs, and she sighs as his finger play with her and his lips close over her nipple. One hand leaves my legs, where she's braced herself, and comes up around his neck.

She's lost in the kiss, her movements becoming more and more frantic, and I brush a finger over the small pucker of her ass, giving just a tiny bit of pressure. She whimpers, and I thrust hard into her pussy as I push past the tight ring of muscles.

She screams, her body going limp and boneless as the orgasm hits her. She grinds down on me, and Luca props her up as the orgasm devastates her. I shove into her again, the sensations sweeping over me until I can't think can't breath can't stop it as I shout, my hand clamped on her hip, holding her tight to me as I follow her over the edge.

Sweet Ruin

Chapter Seventeen

Luca

I step out of the car, and Megan circles to stand between Asher and me as we stare at the house.

"So. Big House. It's an apt name."

"This is where Atti and Nik had their reception," Megan says. "It was a popular place for all of us, in school. Until Grayson died—things changed after that. Scout went downhill pretty fast."

Asher snickers. "His brother's name is Scout?"

"Sister. His little sister. Okay—y'all ready? They know we're here."

I straighten, and Asher's face takes on that studiously bored expression as Megan leads us across the driveway and up the front porch steps.

The door opens before she can knock, and a tall man in a suit, with dark hair and pale blue eyes, steps onto the porch. His gaze is cool as it skates over the two of us, and chills a bit when it settles on Megan. "What are you doing here?"

I stiffen—the question is hostile to the point of being rude, and who the fuck does he think he is, to talk to her like that?

"Nice to see you, too, Dane," Megan says tartly. That's the tone she uses when she's facing off with Kevin, and that annoys me more—because he has her that on edge.

"It's never nice to see the Beauchamp women."

"Who the fuck do you think you are?" Asher snaps, stepping forward. Dane spares him a disinterested look then glances back at Megan.

"I don't care why you're here or that Atti is happy to see you—if you fuck this up for him, I will make sure you and your harpy of a sister will never be happy in this city again."

Her face is white, from shock or anger, I'm not sure which. He straightens away from her as I draw her back into my arms. Blue eyes study me, for the first time seeming to actually notice me.

"I'm not back to stay, Dane. I don't want Branton, and I don't have any desire to hurt Atti—I think Nik did enough there, don't you? I just need my client to talk to him. You can quit protecting him."

He smiles coolly. "You know better. Which of these is your client?"

Asher steps forward. "I am. Asher Knox."

That gets a reaction—Dane blinks, startled, his gaze snapping from Megan to Asher, the hostility draining away to be replaced with shock. "Seriously? Meggy is *your* agent?"

"Don't sound so shocked, Dane," she says dryly.

"Don't call her that," I murmur, and his gaze turns shrewdly assessing.

Then he looks back at Megan. "If Scout starts lusting after these two, you get to explain to my girlfriend why they're not touchable."

Shock stutters across Megan's face. "You're with *Scout?*"

He laughs, a rich rumble, and pushes past us. "Yep. She'll want to have dinner. I'll let her know you're in town."

"Will you be nice?" she mutters, not quite soft enough. Behind us, the Jeep parked to the side of the massive drive way rumbles to life.

"Who the hell was that?" I ask, and I'm surprised I managed to keep my tone civil.

"Dane. Atti's best friend and surrogate brother. And apparently he's dating Scout. He's a bit protective. It's got less to do with me than my sister."

I don't say what I'm thinking. I just squeeze her hand as Asher presses against her back.

She knocks once then walks into the house. It's a warm house, clean and sparsely decorated, but done with the warm touches of a family. And it smells amazing, like spices and chocolate still warm from the oven. I can hear two voices, one a low timbre, the other a higher-pitched laughter.

"Atticus?" Megan calls. There's a heartbeat of silence, and then a man a few years older—late twenties, maybe—

appears at the end of the hall, his green eyes sparkling behind a pair of glasses, hair messy. He's wearing jeans low on his waist, an old band t-shirt, and bare feet.

His smile is wide and genuine, and Megan steps away from us for the first time since last night, almost running into the man's arms.

Atticus Grimes is younger—and better looking—than I expected. I don't know what to do with this.

"Megan, you look fantastic! Have you been home yet?"

"No, we just got in last night—besides, going home this time might be awkward, you know?" She turns and gestures at us.

Atticus' eyes go wide, and startled. "You're Asher Knox."

English nods abruptly, and the disconcerting gaze swings to me. "And you?"

"Luca James."

Confusion crosses his face briefly. No one ever knows the names of male models. It's the curse of our profession.

"I see why you don't want to take them home."

I stiffen and snap, "Why the fuck not?"

Atti smirks. "Because Nik would eat you alive. Or at the very least, she'd try."

Oh.

"Come in, sit down. Megan, we need to talk."

She smiles, a forced expression that almost hurts to look at. "Fine. After lunch?"

We follow Atti into the other room and are greeted by a blonde.

Not just *a* blonde, but a gorgeous one. She's wearing tight jeans and a sweater, her hair pulled into a knot at the nape of her neck. With her big blue eyes and classic good looks, she could give any working actress a run for her money.

"Holy shit, is that Asher Knox?" the girl squeaks, her voice full of disbelief.

I roll a look at him. "Is it always like this?"

"Get used to it," he mutters. He smiles at the girl, who flushes as if realizing that she spoke aloud.

"Sorry," she blurts. "I'm Avery. Atti's fiancée."

Megan smiles. "So you weren't joking. You actually got engaged."

He nods, wrapping an arm around Avery's waist. "You know as well as I do, the marriage ended long before Nik agreed to sign the papers."

"I know of all people to jump back into marriage, you are the last one I expected it from. But then, Dane is dating Scout. Apparently the world is not a place I recognize anymore."

Avery's gaze sweeps to Megan, and I see a shadow pass over her face, as if she's not quite happy to see Megan. Atti shrugs. "Everything changes, Megan. You left to prove that."

I squeeze Megan's hand, a gesture Atticus picks up on, his eyes narrowing minutely.

"Well, come in and sit down," Avery says, her voice nervous, and I let go of Megan, following her into the heart of the house.

Asher

Atticus is disgustingly likable. I listen, not commenting, through a lunch of pasta and chicken tossed in garlic and tomato sauce, served with a thick, warm soup. Avery is quiet, watching us from where she sits at Atti's side, and I see the curious glances he gives her, like he can't quite believe she is being so shy. Megan holds up her end of the conversation, asking all the appropriate questions about life in a small town.

"I've been gone for a few months—but Randall has kept me informed. And as much as we might say differently, the things that make the city tick never change. Classes continue. People fuck. We drink and fight and forgive. That's a small town."

"I know," she murmurs, toying with her fork. "It's why I left."

"But you're back now. For good?" Avery asks, her voice strong for the first time since we sat down.

"No. Asher and Luca are working on *Black Tides*. We came to consult."

Atti's eyes swing to me, sharply assessing. "That movie about Jean Lafitte?"

I nod, and he frowns. "You don't look anything like Jean."

"That's what costume and makeup are for," Megan says, her tone just a little exasperated. "Can you help or not?"

Avery snorts and stands. "I'm getting cake. Megan, do you want any? You just let Atti loose on his favorite subject— we'll be waiting on these three for a while."

She looks a little startled and glances over at us. I nod briefly at her, encouraging her to get to know the quiet girl.

Then I motion to Luca, and we follow Atti down the hall to a spacious bedroom that's been converted into a home office. He grins as we sit down, and from the eager light in his eyes, I have a feeling I'm going to regret asking for his help.

Three hours later, I'm convinced this was the worst idea I've ever had. My head is spinning, and Atti shows no signs of flagging. From the front of the house, the door slaps shut, and Avery shouts Atti's name. A few seconds later, she appears in the doorway, her hair damp from rain and an incredulous look on her face.

"You have not been in here since I left."

Atti blinks at her and shrugs. "Oh my god, Atticus. It's been, like, two hours! Did you even call Scout and tell her that I'm cooking tonight?"

"Um."

She mutters a curse, spinning away to stalk through the house. I stretch, jostling Luca.

"Excuse me for a second," Atti says. He stands and hurries after his grumpy fiancée.

"Where is Megan?" Luca asks, sleepily. He's awake, but I can understand the exhaustion.

"Probably thought Atti chopped up our bodies and fed them to the gators and is happily on her way back to California."

He laughs, and I stand. My back pops, and I stifle a groan.

We're in the hallway when Luca stops me, and I hear them talking.

Luca

Megan's voice is off—thick with sleep and something I'm not sure I can assess. Not without seeing her, and she's firmly out of sight.

"I like them. Good guys," Atticus says. "I don't think they heard anything after the first ten minutes, but it was polite to listen anyway."

"Atti, you kept them locked up for two hours!"

He laughs, and then, "How long have you been with them?"

"I met Luca when I got to LA. He was my roommate. Asher's been a client—"

"I meant, *with them.*"

There's a moment of silence, and then, her voice, stiff and colder than I've ever heard it. "I don't know what the hell you're talking about."

My stomach hallows out, and I take a step back. No. She didn't—she misunderstood. Asher's hands catch me, supporting me as my world, the neatly ordered plan I've put together, the dreams of a life outside the shadow cast by Dylan, gets tossed out the fucking window.

"Asher and Luca are friends—clients, and good friends. But I'm not with them."

"But, you guys seem so close," Avery protests.

"Not that kind of close," she says, disdainfully.

I want to run. I want to scream. I want to demand an explanation, a reason she would say that about us. Logic says she's protecting herself—and us. A triad isn't the most conventional of relationships, and it's still new enough that can I really blame her for denying us?

Yes. I can and I do. She didn't even hesitate. There was no judgment in Atti's voice—and she still denied us like we were nothing.

"Let's go," Asher says softly. His grip on my hip tightens, just a little, enough that I'm shaken from my daze and forced to look at him. His eyes are worried and demanding. I nod at the questions lingering there and force a tired smile. "Fine, English. I'm fine."

He leans down, kissing me quickly, and we walk out of the hallway.

Atticus and Avery are standing in the kitchen, and Megan is by the bar, looking like she just rolled off the couch, uncomfortable as hell.

Her gaze darts to us, and I see a hint of pleading in her gaze. "We need to go," is all I say.

She nods and turns to smile at Atticus. "Thank so much for your time. I'm sure it was more than enough."

Avery snorts. English is together enough to shake Atti's hand, and then we're out the door and I can catch my breath, just a little. Megan looks startled as I push past her and slide into the back seat. Asher gives her a slightly apologetic look and ducks in behind me.

We're halfway back to the hotel before Megan kills the radio and frowns at us in the rearview mirror. "Okay, what's wrong?"

"Nothing," I snap, and she laughs. She *laughs.*

Asher squeezes my knee, but doesn't address Meg's question. She huffs. "I can't fix it if you won't talk to me," she says.

"Sweetheart, you couldn't fix this if I did talk," I snap.

She goes still, her eyes wide and hurt. How dare she? What fucking right does she have to be hurt? None. None at all.

"What the hell do you think this is, Megan? Do you think I walked away from Hollywood to chase you here for a coupla fucks? A chance to have Knox suck my dick?"

She flinches, and Asher speaks up. "Easy, Luc."

"Fuck that," I snarl. "You heard her. We *both* heard her. She said we're nothing. Friends." I lean forward, my lips right at Megan's ear, and hiss, "I don't fuck my friends the way I did you."

"What the hell did you want me to say," she demands, her voice shaking. "Tell him I'm with you both? Because, you know, that would be killer publicity."

"He's your fucking brother-in-law, Megan," I shout, unable to keep it in anymore. "If you can't trust him, who *can* you trust? Or do you think we'll be able to keep it a secret forever? Do you plan to be seen on Knox's arm and come home to both of us? Do you *really* think we can keep it from the entire press when we go home?"

She doesn't say anything, and I know. A sick feeling grips my stomach. I sit back, trying not to think about it. Trying to ignore the fact that this thing, this wonderful new, fragile thing will be gone.

I will lose them both.

Sweet Ruin

Chapter Eighteen

Megan.

Luca is walking like he's injured, and Asher is hovering over him like a sexy, overgrown mother hen.

Really, who would have thought Asher Knox, Hollywood heartthrob, would turn out to be such a sweet softie?

"Luca," I say, softly, as the elevator chimes. The doors to my floor open, and I step out.

They don't follow me.

My stomach swoops, and I can feel tears pricking at the back of my eyelids. I knew, I knew I would lose them. But I'm not ready to. Not yet. Not like this, with him so angry.

For a wild moment, I want to take it all back, and I want to throw my phone down—and then I remember that this is the best case scenario. There is no way to walk away from this without them furious.

So I take a step, and another, until the elevator swishes shut behind me, and I'm at my hotel room door. Until I'm inside, and the darkness that was so welcoming, the bed that was so warm—is no comfort at all.

I wake up alone. They haven't crept in and filled the empty spaces around me. After the time on the road, it feels odd, being so utterly alone.

A light blinks in the dark room, and my phone vibrates again, a harsh noise that jars me to wakefulness.

I glance at the text message.

I'm too sober and too sad to deal with Kevin right now. I groan and silence the phone.

Why did I agree to this—why did I offer it, in the first place? Because it was the only way to keep my job, and that job was the only thing I had to prove that I wasn't a huge fuck up.

Asher, Luca—they didn't matter. They *couldn't* matter.

I look at the message again and bite down on my tongue to keep from screaming.

Kevin: **Where's the press you promised? Everyone wants to know where Knox is.**

Me: **I said I needed time. Don't worry—you won't be able to miss this, when it hits.**

He doesn't respond, which is fine. I don't want to deal with my uncle.

Frankly, I don't want to deal with any of my family.

Asher

"What the hell just happened?"

Luca drops across one of the full-sized beds and stares at the ceiling blankly. If he knows I'm here at all, he's doing a damn good job of pretending I'm not.

I stare at him for a second then retreat to the bathroom, stripping out of my clothes and climbing into a hot shower.

I understand his anger and shock. It stings, more than I want to think about, that she didn't even hesitate before denying anything between us. It's not surprising—but it hurts. The door creaks open, and Luca stands there, looking fragile and broken—there is no sign of the strong man who has been so very clear about what he wants.

That hurts, too. That she can break him so easily.

I pull the curtain back a little, a silent invitation. Luca doesn't waste any time, shedding his clothes and stepping into the spray. There is a surreal moment when I think about the fact that I am naked in a shower with another guy, but it fades as I tilt his chin up and study the bruised look in his eyes.

"This isn't the end, Luc," I say softly.

"So what if it's not? I can't do this knowing she'll end it before we get home—I can't let myself fall in love with you if I have to give you up."

His words echo through the little bathroom, and I shiver, absorbing them. "You already love her."

He nods, a bitter look on his face. "I do."

"And me?"

Surprise flicks across his face, and I lean down, kissing him lightly, a feather soft touch. "What about me?"

"I—"

I reach between us, cupping his erection, and he groans. "How do you feel about me, Luca?" I ask, my voice a soft tease. He arches into my touch, and I laugh. I let him go, and twist him so I'm pressed against his back. "How. Do. You. Feel."

"Asher," he whimpers.

"I'm only asking," I say, stroking his erection slowly, my tone almost conversational, "because I'm falling in love with you."

He gasps, his cock jerking, and I smirk. "I wouldn't be here," he gasps, "if I didn't love you."

Luca twists, staring at me over his shoulder, and I see nothing but stark honesty in his gaze. "Both of you. I love you both."

And there it is. The words we haven't said, not in the thousand miles on the road or the flirting or fooling around. All his cards are on the table, and it hits me hard, that he has more invested in this than any of us.

I want to chase that thought, but I want to make the sadness in his eyes go away more. So I thrust against him, and he moans, pushing his ass back against my cock.

"I've never been with a guy, Luc," I admit, and he looks over his shoulder again. "Not tonight, Luc. But soon." I kiss him again, and it's like a cue, as he moves, his cock thrusting into my grip on him. His eyes are open, when he comes. Watching me. Full of vulnerability that leaves me shaken. I slowly release him and move to step away.

"If she leaves, you'll go with her."

His word make me still. His shoulders hunch, and I hug him. There is nothing sexual in the touch, nothing more than an offer of comfort. It isn't much—but right now, as he leans into me, it's all I have to offer.

Because the truth is I don't know what I will do, if I have to choose one of them. The idea is foreign, strange—they are a package deal, a pair.

"So let's get dressed and check out the town. There has to be something to do, and it'll give you some time to cool off," I say. Luca nods against my shoulder, and I give him a final squeeze before I let go.

We end up on Main Street. In a city the size of Branton—which is to say, tiny—there aren't a lot of places to wander. But it's charming, in a too sweet, Southern sort of way. It reminds me of home, if through a distorted lens. Classy boutiques and barber shops and a tack store line Main Street. There are a few small restaurants and the café Megan dragged us into when we got into town.

It's a college town, and for the first time, I feel nervous—what if someone recognizes me? Luca bumps me with his elbow, an innocuous touch, and I glance at him. His gaze is amused, knowing. "The café?"

It had dark corners. Good place for making out and avoiding attention. Both attractive options in a town like Branton, or any college town, really. I nod.

Its quiet inside Hill of Beans—apparently Thursday afternoons aren't peak business hours. A thin young man with an infectious smile is standing behind the counter, a little girl sitting in a bouncy chair in his line of sight. Jeffery is nowhere to be seen.

"Ah. Dirty chai and hot tea. Right?" the man chirps, and Luca freezes at my side. Maybe it wasn't a good idea, coming here. The man looks up again and flashes another smile. "Jeff doesn't gossip. But even he'll mention an a-list actor and one of the finest models working walking through the shop. I'm surprised Meg isn't with y'all—he mentioned that too."

There's a smirk in his eyes, something that tells me this smart, fast-talking young man has no ill intentions. He hurries about making the drinks, tosses a couple blackberry scones on a plate, and slides the lot of it across the counter to us. "You can probably get some privacy upstairs—there's a few tables up there, but it doesn't get a lot of traffic.

He nods at the thin staircase, and I glance at Luca. He shrugs and heads toward it with our drinks. I look at the barista before I follow, and the man smiles. "I'm Jason. And no one will bother you. Should I tell her where you are, if she comes in?"

I ponder that—if she wants us to be around, shouldn't we let her?

I nod, once, and follow Luca.

Luca

I sit on the love seat—Jason didn't mention when he directed us here that it was only two loveseats and a single oversized recliner, all spaced to give couples an air of intimacy.

Asher places the scones on the table, and I sip cautiously at my dirty chai, watching him from under my eyelashes. He's got something on his mind—and for once, I don't think it's that he's fooling around with a dude.

"What do you want to do?" he asks, and I know without asking what he's talking about.

Megan's presence is felt like a wound, a warm, feisty spitfire that is painfully absent.

"I can't force her to accept this. I want her to. But I can't make her do something she's decided not to."

Asher laughs and shakes his head. "Dude. You talked me into being with you. You could talk an Eskimo into buying ice."

"I don't want to 'talk her into' it. I want her to be with us because she wants to be—because she can't imagine being with anyone else. Because life without us would be awful and broken."

I stare at him, and he flushes, looking away irritably. "What?"

"You just throw it all out there, don't you. This is what you want. This is what you feel. This isn't a you/me thing. It's an us. You put so much out there, and to hell with what other people think."

I sigh, thinking about that day. Fuck it. Why not tell him? "I never got to grieve, when Dylan died. Everyone knew he was with Sun, and I got the usual amount of 'your best friend died' platitudes. But my team, my other friends, hell even my parents—they couldn't understand why I didn't bounce back from his death, why I quit playing football. I couldn't tell them—what would I say? Dylan was dead, and everyone knew he was head over heels for Sun. So mentioning that we were together, that the three of us were—it wasn't an option. She tried, you know, to help. But people started talking, about us being together, and we had to cool that off."

He looks at me, a look of startled horror, and I offer him a tight smile.

"I dropped out. Got so depressed I couldn't think about school or anything. I lost my scholarship, and I didn't even care. I was a mess." I take a deep breath and stare into my chai, trying to focus on that and not the nightmares of my past. It's gone—done. A life I beat and moved past. "I tried to kill myself on his birthday. Took a drug cocktail and a drank a bottle of Grey Goose. I should have died—I wanted too, and I would have."

"Sun?" he whispers, softly.

"She came over, wanting to talk. I was passed out, convulsing. She called 911, got me to the hospital and help. My parents didn't know what to do—and without knowing what I had lost, they couldn't help. Sun told them, while I was on psych hold."

He makes a sharp noise, and I smirk. "No, it was ok. They didn't really get it—still don't, actually. They hope it's a thing I'll outgrow when I find the right woman."

"You don't think so?"

"I've tried, man. I tried girls, I tried guys. And it's never been awful—ok, that one week with the girl on *Days?* That was awful." He laughs, a warm noise, leaning back into his seat. His arm brushes mine, and I feel electricity spring between us, a live current of desire. "But it never felt right. It wasn't complete. It's not about the sex, Ash. I know a lot of people think it's about the kink, and I'll say the sex is amazing—I love that part. But it's this. It's you knowing I'm upset, and being here, talking me through it. It's knowing that she'll keep us in line, and when you hit one of your moods, we can drag you back. It's falling asleep to the sound of you breathing, and her pressed between us. It's not sex—it's the entire fucking package. I know what that's like—that was normal for me, and whatever people say about it, it's what makes me work. I can't do long term single relationships."

"No monogamy for you, huh," he grunts, and I stiffen and look at him.

"Oh no. Monogamy is a given. I'm with you and her. Which means I'm not with anyone else—and I expect it from both of you."

He nods, slowly, his eyes trained on me.

"So if you're so determined to be with her and me, why are we here and not with her?"

"Because I can't hide, Asher. And neither of you wants everything that will come with being a public triad."

He frowns, but doesn't debate that. Instead, "If we want this bad enough, we'll make it work."

"It doesn't matter what we want, if she doesn't want us."

Asher smiles, then, an arrogant tilt to his lips and a lazy look in his eyes that sets my blood on fire, and I find myself leaning into him.

"You've been her best friend for almost two years. She's been working with me, almost living in my house, for six months. We both want her—and she knows it. And she's here, waiting for us. Now, after two years of waiting for the endgame, are you really going to walk because she threw up a road block? Come on, man. Step up. Show us both just how far you'll push."

It's a taunt, a deliberate one. I know it is, and I still can't help that my hackles rise. I glare at him. "Seriously, English?"

He leans into me, stealing a quick kiss. "Come on, Luc. Fight for us. I will."

Megan

I stare at them from the corner of the staircase. They're wrapped up in each other, lost in whatever they're talking about. Asher leans his head against Luc's shoulder. My hand, holding my phone, twitches, calling up the camera. Luc laughs at something Asher murmurs, and twists to drop a kiss on his hair.

And I snap the pic, quickly, then drop my phone into my purse. It's locked. They won't know it was me. Without giving myself time to think, I backtrack down the stairs. Jason's eyes go wide when he sees me, and he opens his mouth to say something. I shake my head quickly and beckon to him. With a last glance at the baby—and really, I need details on that—he follows me outside.

On the windy, cool side walk, he arches an eyebrow. "What are you doing? Those two are waiting on you."

I look at him sharply and see it—he knows. I don't know how he knows, but it's there. He knows exactly what's going on, and I don't know how to deal with that.

"I don't know what to do, Jase. I—this wasn't part of the plan. *They* weren't part of the plan."

His gaze softens a tiny bit. Sympathy, coating the steel. Whatever he says, I won't like it. But that's always been Jason— the bitter truth, because sometimes, life is bitter.

"Megan, those boys adore you. One look at them, I could tell that. Hell, Jeff could, and he's about as obtuse as an ox. Maybe, sweetheart, it's time to look away from the plan you've had and look at what you've got."

I shake my head, hard. "What does that ever do? I'd end up like Nik—miserable. In a marriage to a man I hate. Cheating just to get his attention."

He snorts. "Atticus isn't with that harpy—and yes, I know. She's your sister. But she's a bitch. And you, despite all your fears that you'll turn out that way, are nothing like her." His gaze narrows. "Or you weren't, when you left."

That stings. More than I like, because I know about the picture in my phone, the picture I could use to secure my job—and destroy this fragile thing we're building.

"I'm scared." I whisper. "I don't know what to do. I know what they want, and Jase, I'm scared. I want it, but I want my career. Whatever I choose, I'm losing." I stare at him, this boy I grew up with. The kid I ran to when Nikki got too insane to deal with, the one who wanted to hang out with me because of me, and not my sister. The only guy who didn't seem to notice I had a sister.

Of course, Jase has been out since we were in eighth grade.

"Megan, this isn't a hard decision," he says, turning back to open the door. A low laugh filters out—Luca—and the squeal of the baby. His gaze softens. "You choose the thing you can't imagine life without."

I end up back at the hotel, alone. I stare at the picture for a long time, and something—god only knows what—keeps me from hitting send. It would be so easy, to cement my career. To let Kevin know how cutthroat I can be.

He doesn't believe it. He never has.

The phone rings, startling me, and I stare as the picture of Luca and Asher vanishes, replaced by my sister's smiling face. I swallow my sigh—it was only a matter of time until she realized I was home.

Twenty-four hours is a damn good run, if you ask me.

"Hey," I say, trying to summon some enthusiasm to put in my voice.

"Why on earth are you in Branton? Why didn't you tell me you were coming home? I would have picked you up."

"I drove in, Nik. And it's for work, so I didn't want to bother you. I can't hang out."

She's quiet, and then her voice changes, subtly. Takes on that sexy edge I'm used to hearing from Nik. "What kind of work?"

"The kind that comes with NDA's and bodyguards," I say, too tired for this. "Nik, no. No intros, no sex. They just came to do some research."

She laughs. "In Branton? What on earth do we have that an actor would need to research?"

I'm quiet, and then—because it's Branton, and *nothing* stays secret, I tell her. "They're working on *Black Tides*."

Her tone loses the sex, goes shrill. "You came home to see *Atticus?*"

Ah yes, this is why I've been avoiding her. One of the many reasons. "No, Nik. I came here to let my clients relax before they start filming. If we happen to have an expert on hand, yes, I'll use him. It has nothing to do with you."

"He's my ex-husband," she snaps.

"Not my fault," I shoot back, coldly. "That was no one's decision but your own. Now. Are we going to do this, or would you like to grab lunch—and be civil about it?"

She's quiet, a startled silence. I don't usually take the offensive—I let her run all over me. That's what I've been doing since we were little girls and she was pulling my braids.

I never told Daddy. And she knew I never would. I wanted her approval too much.

"Fine," she huffs. "Tomorrow, at Maggie's."

"See you at eleven."

She hangs up without saying goodbye, and I wonder if she thinks I'll bring the boys. I wonder if she knows, yet, which boys I brought home. I'll never hear the end of it, if she does. But I'm done backing down when my sister wants something—and I refuse to share them with her. I might not know what I want, but I do know it's not that.

Without letting myself think, I creep out of my room, up the stairs, and slip the spare key to my room under the boys' door.

Then I retreat to my room and curl up in the middle of the too big bed, alone.

It takes a long time to fall asleep.

Sweet Ruin

Chapter Nineteen

Asher

The morning comes early here—sounds from people on the street trickling in, the putter of housekeeping in the hall.

Luca is sleeping on his side of the bed, sprawled on his stomach, his arms stretched above his head.

It doesn't surprise me, the story he shared last night. It should, because he's so confident and sure of himself now—but that kind of confidence is something you earn, and he did. He earned it by going through hell.

I lean over and brush a kiss over his forehead. "I'm going for a run."

He mumbles, "Fucking show off."

I laugh and slip from the bed. In the bathroom, I change quickly and tug on my shoes. Luca is already snoring again when I let the hotel door shut softly behind me.

There was a park, across the street, and I saw runners jogging on what looks like a loop around the university.

So I might get lost, but I have some idea of what I'm doing—and it's a tiny town. How long could I possibly be lost for?

She's in the lobby, wearing a pair of running pants and a form fitting coat, her red hair pulled into a tight pony tail. She looks adorable and gorgeous, in a way that is utterly touchable. Not the way she looks at home, in her pencil skirts and business suits and perfectly styled hair. Here she is comfortable, and I love seeing her like that.

She turns, and her eyes widen as she freezes. I have a few seconds to decide what to do, and then I walk across the lobby to stand in front of her.

"Run with me?"

She looks nervous, and grateful. But she doesn't say anything—just licks her lips nervously and nods.

I lead us outside, and she points at the loop I had noticed. We walk toward it and stop, stretching silently. After about five minutes, I straighten and bounce on my toes. Megan flashes a look in my direction, and then she breaks into a smooth, even jog down the pavement.

We don't talk. I let her set the pace, and it's good, the cool morning air brisk in my nose and the city coming to life around me. The sound of our feet and the rasp of her breath. The delicious ache in my legs that I've missed.

It's exactly what I need—and her lush ass is the perfect scenery.

We make two silent loops before she slows the pace, and I know she's ready to talk.

"You didn't come to my room," she pants.

"No. Luca needs some time, lovely. Needs to process what you said and what it means for us."

"That isn't fair."

I shrug, my breath settling. This pace isn't punishing, and I'm able to talk almost without effort. "Neither is denying anything happened, without giving us a chance to talk about it. That was harsh—you have to admit that."

"Maybe it was wrong. But we hadn't discussed, and it came out of nowhere. He's my brother-in-law, Asher. What was I supposed to tell him?"

"He wasn't judging you. That's what you're afraid of, and there was nothing there. Denying us like that—Luca can't handle it. He had to go through it when Dylan died, and I won't be part of doing it to him again."

She stops, so abruptly she has to hurt herself, and it takes me a few steps to realize she's no longer at my side.

"What do you mean by that?" she says, her voice just a tiny bit shrill and uncertain.

I tell her, briefly. None of the gory details, but enough to tell her how serious this is.

"He needs commitment. You think we have a lot to lose, Megs, and we do. I know that. But Luca had already lost so much, and he chose us to rebuild with. I can't betray that kind of trust," I say tiredly.

"I...I didn't know. He's never said anything."

"Why would he?" I ask, not cruelly. "It's tied to Dylan, and he doesn't talk about that."

She blinks hard. "I fucked up, didn't I?"

I nod. "Yeah, sweetheart. You did."

She flinches. I grab her, pulling her into a hug despite the sweat covering us.

"It's fixable, Megs. We are fixable. He wants this, and I want this."

As I say it, I realize how true it is. I want this—with all the broken, fucked-up, messy pieces that it brings. I want her, all steel and silk and insecurities, and him, with his demons and laughter and cocky assurance that this is right.

I want it all.

"I want my career, Ash. And if I'm with you both, I'll be a laughing stock. I need to prove I'm more than that—that I can be more than my sister."

My gaze narrows. There she is again—that sister that keeps popping up. The one Atti married and divorced; the one who visits Megan, but I haven't met. Who is this girl, and why does she have such a hold on Megan?

"You would throw away what we have—what we could be, to prove something to this sister?" I ask, not sure I honestly understand her.

But she bites her lip and nods, and my stomach drops.

Without letting myself think, I shove my fingers into her hair, pulling her ponytail out and letting red silk spill over my hand as I drag her close, closing the distance with my lips.

She's stiff for less than a heartbeat, and then she melts against me, her arms coming up to wrap around my neck and tug me closer. I nip at her lip, and she gasps, opening for me. I take the invitation, slipping past her lips to tangle with her tongue, stroking it with a slow slide as my hand slips down to cup her hip, drawing her into me. I know she can feel my erection, but I thrust into her. She rewards me with a moan, grinding into me. I want to scoop her up and take her back to Luca. Want to worship her body and imprint myself so deeply, there is no way to separate herself from us.

But that won't work. So I slowly release her, soften my kiss until its chaste and she's breathing almost normal, leaning against me. She's almost calm.

I let her go and step back.

"I want to meet her."

Megan's eyes go wide, and her mouth opens, already forming the denial. I step into her, catching her shoulders and ducking to stare into her eyes. "This isn't just you, Megan. This is three of us. If you will throw us away because of this girl, we at least deserve the chance to see what we're up against. We deserve the chance to fight for us."

Her eyes well with tears, and she shakes her head. "It will change things, Ash. Nik always changes things. It's not a good idea."

I nod. "Then don't come back to us. Don't do that to me and Luca."

It's a gauntlet, and I can't breathe while I watch her process the words and my meaning, her eyes going wide and hurt.

I see when she relents, the way her shoulders slump, and she nods. She looks impossibly broken.

"Ok. I'm meeting her for lunch."

I nod and take her hand. "Then let's get Luca up."

Luca

I wake up when he steps into the room. I've been hovering for some time on that edge between sleep and wakefulness, and the noise of him walking into the room, even quietly, pushes me firmly into the land of wakefulness.

"Where have you been?" I ask, blinking sleepily.

Asher drops down next to me on the bed. "I got you coffee."

I push up on my elbows, staring at him with a brow lifted. "What are you trying to talk me into, Knox?"

"Lunch," he answers promptly. "With Megan and her sister."

I shake my head. "Not yet."

"Yes. Yet. Look, you want her? You're going to have to fight for her a little—show her that you're serious."

"I followed her halfway across the fucking country!"

"This sister is the problem, man. She's a complete mess when it comes to her—she almost fell apart when she was talking about her this morning."

I sit up abruptly, and Asher curses as the coffee splashes his chest.

Mmm. Bare chest.

Wait. "You *saw* her this morning?"

He sighs and puts the coffee down. Retreats to the bathroom where he turns on the shower. "Yeah. She was going for a run, so we ran together. I know you're pissed, man. So am I. But if we want to make this work, we have to actually communicate with her—tell her why we're pissed and figure out how to make this work long term. We know she has hang ups—this sister is one of them. So let's show her why it's an obstacle we can overcome."

He's using we—talking about us like it's a given, a known and accepted fact of life. That's different. I crawl out of bed and stand in the doorway of the bathroom. The shower billows steam out, framing him as he shaves quickly. On his neck, there is a red mark—my teeth made it.

"You want to fight for us," I say.

Asher lowers the razor and smirks at me. "Idiot. Of course I do. You're the only thing I've got to distract the screaming girls."

He winks and I laugh. "Fine. You win. We'll go have lunch with Megan and her sister."

Asher finishes shaving then comes to me. His skin is soft and smooth, and I can't help but catch his jaw as he dips in for a kiss. "Get ready to go, English," I murmur, stepping back. "We have to go convince the woman we love that she's being an idiot."

Chapter Twenty

Megan

Asher promised to bring Luca, but I didn't realize how doubtful I was until the elevator doors glide open and there they both stand. I tremble a little as Luca eyes me, face blank behind his sunglasses. Asher gives me an encouraging smile, and I step in, the door shutting and closing all the awkward tension into the area around us.

Luca isn't talking, staring doggedly at his feet. Asher shifts, drawing my attention, and nods briefly at Luca.

I flush, but murmur what I should have said yesterday. "I'm sorry."

He looks up, and I meet his eyes over the rim of his sunglasses. He looks tired, like he didn't sleep, worried. Everything that makes me want to reach up and soothe away his worry lines, and I can't. Because he might acknowledge me, but there is still an ocean of distance between us.

The elevator stops, and the doors open. Asher lets out the breath it feels like all of us are holding, and Luca steps past me.

But his fingers brush mine as he does, and it's enough to make me think I can maybe fix this mess.

Some things, you spend your entire life trying to change. The way you are perceived, and the places that you come from. The acceptance—or lack of it—from family. Things that *can* be changed, if you work hard enough, for long enough.

Some things, like Maggie's, can't be.

It smells exactly like it did when I first came here, as a little girl, bright eyed and confused by the Deep South. The scent of creole and gumbo, cornbread and fried chicken fills the air. I slide a quick glance at the boys as they take in the ratty wooden tables and cheap plastic chairs.

The place has rolls of paper towels on the tables, for crying out loud.

I don't pause at the hostess stand—LouAnn has known me since I was tiny, and she knows my sister. Instead, I bypass the empty lectern and lead the boys to a back booth.

Nikki Beauchamp is sitting on one side, wearing a sweater dress, her blonde hair pulled over one shoulder. Because I know my sister, I know that there are black tights and hooker boots to match the silver sweater.

I hear the boys inhale at the sight of her, and my heart drops a little.

"Hey, Nik. Sorry I'm late. They wanted to come with me."

Nikki looks up from her phone, and I see the shock, there for a perfect moment, and then gone, so quickly I wonder if the boys even noticed.

"Meggy. Sweetheart, you have to introduce your friends."

I bristle. "Clients, Nik. This is Luca James, and I'm sure you recognize Asher Knox. Two clients I'm working with—and yes, dear friends."

Luca gives me a quick searching look, and Nik smiles, all sex and seduction. Of course, she would be. "Come sit by me," she almost purrs.

I grit my teeth, choking on my protest. Luca gives her a slow smile, one I would know anywhere—the one he uses when he and Sun seduce girls in the clubs.

"I'd love to."

I make a tiny noise, something Nik doesn't even notice, and Luca's eyes dart to me, a little bit mocking.

I force myself to slide in across from my sister, and Asher drops next to me, his leg pressed against mine, warm and comforting.

Nik, not surprisingly, is ignoring me. All of her attention is focused on Luca. "I think I've heard of you," she says, softly, leaning into him.

Asher laughs, softly, but not so softly that Nik misses it. She shoots a dark look at him, and I sigh. "He's a male model,

Nik. No one has heard of him, and everyone is intimately aware of his abs."

"And the v," Asher adds, straight faced. I giggle. Nik's face twists in annoyance.

"So what are you doing here?" she demands, abandoning seduction for the moment. Our waitress arrives, and I wait as she takes our drink orders. Nik is watching me, and I duck behind my menu—a menu I've had memorized since I was fourteen and worked here for a summer.

"What's good?" Asher asks. I glance at him and then Luca.

"I'll order for us," I say, dropping the menu back onto the table. Luca's lips twitch, but neither argues with me. Nik is staring at me, a half smile on her lips. It pisses me off. I know that look.

It says I'm nothing. I barely register to her. My lips thin, and I turn away from her to focus on the waitress as she returns with our drinks.

Nik orders a salad with chicken breast. Her mouth forms a small o of surprise when I order two plates of fried chicken, a large bowl of gumbo, a dish of red beans and rice, and dirty shrimp and grits.

"All of this on the same check?" the waitress asks.

I shake my head. "No. The boys are with me."

Asher laughs, and the waitress gives him an indulgent smile as she walks away. He slides an arm around my waist, tugging me against him as we lean back in the booth.

"So. You're done with Hollywood, then?" Nik says, and she sounds almost normal.

"No. We're only here for a few weeks—the boys have a film, I told you that."

"And you're going back with them."

"I'm going back to my career and my life there, yes."

She gives me an annoyed look. "I still don't understand what the whole point of this is, Meggy. Daddy would give you a job, if you want to work."

"I don't want the job you decided you were too good for," I say softly. "I don't want to stay in a city where I'll never be more than your sister."

She flinches. Have I ever put it out there like that?

"I didn't realize you hated me so much," Nik says stiffly.

"We should go," Luca says, the first thing he's said since we sat down.

"Please don't," I say. This needs to be said—it's been needed for years, and I've been too afraid of saying it. I look at my sister, with her classic beauty and injured dignity and the smiles men can't seem to resist. "Nik, I don't hate you—I never did. It's hard, though. Being your half-sister, in a town like Branton? Everyone knew you. Everyone loved you. You have no idea what that's like, to live in a constant shadow. To be compared, every time you do something, to the sister you'll never live up to. It's exhausting. I went halfway across the country to try and get away from that shadow."

"I wasn't even in Branton when you were in college."

"Do you think that matters?" I demand. "This city remembers *everything.*"

"So you decided that you should hook up with two men as an attempt to be different from me?" she says, her tone scornful.

I laugh. "Well, it's not *that* different, given how Atti caught you."

She pales and whispers, "You bitch."

My phone vibrates, and I glance at it before dropping it onto the table. "Maybe. Maybe I am. But I'm also done. I've spent years trying to earn your approval and to show this city that I'm not you, and I'm over it. I have a life—one I love—and a job that I'm good at, and I don't need anyone's approval for that. I have Luca and Asher. I don't need anything else."

"You mean, you don't need me," she says, her voice sharp. "Because we both know you need Uncle Kevin. Without him, you wouldn't have access to such pretty"—she eyes Asher, and I stiffen, furious—"clients."

"Back off, Nik," I say softly. "They're mine."

She smirks, and I shake my head. "This one likes me. Take the time traveler. I like models."

"Are you serious?" I demand. "He's a person, Nikki! They both are."

"And we're a package, love," Asher says.

"Boys, can y'all give me a minute?" I say abruptly.

Luca and Asher hesitate, and then Knox nods and stands. "Come on, Luc. We'll get lunch to go."

I wait for them to walk away, and I look at my sister. I used to want so much, when I looked at her—acceptance and pride. Hell, I'd have been happy with recognition. She's staring at me with that infuriating mix of cool superiority. I laugh, softly. "I'll never be good enough for you. I will never be more than a crying kid Daddy brought home that you didn't want to deal with."

Her eyes widen, and then she shrugs. "It is what it is, Meggy. I don't know why you fight it."

"Because I wanted you to love me," I say and give her a twisted smile. "Stupid, right? I want your approval, and I want to show you that I can be more than that little girl. That's why I left home—because I couldn't while I was here. And I—" I cut off abruptly, a thought hitting me suddenly.

"What?" she demands.

"I don't want to be you." I whisper. "Or Kevin."

Nik frowns, but I don't bother to explain myself. How can I? Instead, I scramble out of the booth and hurry toward the front of the restaurant, where Asher and Luca are waiting for me.

I run into Luca's arms, and he closes them around me, catching me to him without an ounce of hesitation. This—this is what home feels like. His arms around me, and Asher's presence only a few inches away, the scent of laundry and shampoo and Lacoste in my nose. A scent I will always associate with Luca and his easy smiles and long days in the back of a car, traveling across the country.

"I'm sorry," I choke out, and he shudders, his grip on me tightening for a second. He kisses my hair and loosens his grip enough that I can take a step back, just a short one. "I'm sorry—I want this. I know we have to talk, figure out how it will work, but—I don't want to throw us away." I take a deep breath. "I'm going to quit the agency."

Both of them freeze, and I see shock in their eyes. "Megan. Are you sure that's what you want?"

I nod. "I'll tell you when we get home. Come on."

Asher pushes open the door, and I start to follow them. "Meggy!"

I hesitate at my sister's call. She walks up, and even now, she's sleek elegance and unhurried grace. "You left your phone," she says simply.

She looks past me, to where Asher and Luca are. And then she smiles at me. "I hope you are happy, Megan. I really do."

Then she turns and walks away, and for the first time in I don't know how long, being dismissed by my sister doesn't sting.

Sweet Ruin

Chapter Twenty One

Luca

I don't know what happened—what changed in such a short amount of time. But I don't want to question it—I'm happy to just take Megan and Asher on their terms.

"Her sister is pretty horrible." I mutter to Ash, watching them. Megan looks startled, but not upset. Which is why I'm here and not across the parking lot, dragging her away from the blonde bitch she calls a sister.

"Half-sisters. Pretty sure there's a story there."

"But will she tell us?"

"If she won't, I bet Atticus will. Avery invited us for dinner tonight."

I glance at him from the corner of my eye. "What time tonight?"

His expression grows lazy and content, desire sparking in his blue eyes. "Hours from now."

Megan approaches us, and I let her slide into the car as Asher circles to the driver side.

"What did she want?"

"I forgot my phone," she says absently. "Are you still mad at me?"

I blink. "Of course not. I was never mad."

Asher snorts.

"Ok, I was mad," I amend, "but mostly I was hurt. I don't want us to be something you can so easily dismiss. I understand that it's difficult—and we'll figure out how to deal with the publicity of such a untraditional relationship. But we need to do it together—so no one gets hurt when this shit happens. I can't do it."

"You don't have to. We'll figure this out," she says.

I believe her.

"We're supposed to be at Atticus' at seven for dinner."

Megan nods, shifting nervously. She's nibbling at her lip, propped against the dresser.

"What just happened, Megan?" I ask. Asher, sitting behind me on the bed, nudges me with his foot, and I bat him away irritably. I need answers—there are too many questions, and the change is too abrupt. I want to trust it. I want to believe we're fine and there will be no more road bumps.

But I'm not an idiot.

"Have you ever wanted something for so long, and you fight for it—and then one day, you wake up and realize that the thing you wanted has turned you into the one thing you've never wanted to be?"

There's a moment of silence, and then, "Cryptic Megan is cryptic," Asher says dryly.

She laughs, a startled noise, and he grins. "Just tell us, sweetheart. No judgments here."

"I wanted to prove I wasn't my sister. I wanted to be more than her and this tiny town. Because I wasn't from here— I moved here when my mother died, and our father was saddled with me."

"Megs," I say, and she shakes her head quickly.

"No, it's fine. I was a little girl, and Daddy was always good to me. But Nik was his princess, and she hated my intrusion. I just wanted her to like me, and she couldn't stand the sight of me." I shake my head. "So I decided to be everything she wasn't. If she was the small town darling, I wanted to make it in the big city. If she refused to work, I wanted a career. If she got married right out of high school, I wanted nothing to do with relationships."

"I don't understand how you are becoming her?"

"I'm not," she says then shakes her head. "I don't want to ruin this. And I will. I'll do something—for Kevin or my own career, or just because I'm angry and I'll lash out and I'll destroy us. It's what I do. It's what Nik does, and I'm her sister, after all."

"But this isn't just you, Megan," I say. "It's all of us. You can't ruin this by yourself."

She looks miserable and shakes her head. "I could. You say that I can't, but—you have no idea. Kevin wants me to report on y'all."

There's dead silence, broken only by the hum of the heater. She won't even look up at us. And I don't know what to do with this information—because she's right.

This. This could ruin us, before we even have a chance.

"But you didn't," Asher says, and his voice is strong.

"I told him I would, Ash. Do you understand what I'm saying? I knew what was happening between us, and I knew if I waited, I could use it."

"Did you?" I whisper.

"*No!*" she almost shouts. "I don't want to ruin us. Don't you get it? That's why I'm quitting. Because if I quit, I can't. At least not that way."

A knot of tension unravels, and I glance back at Asher.

Asher

She didn't betray us. She didn't.

"Y'all would be better off without me," she whispers, and my heart jerks.

"No," I say, coming to my feet. I step past Luca and take her hands. "That's off the table, pet. We're in this together. I love you. Both of you."

"Leaving you isn't an option. And if you ruin this? We'll put us back together. Do you understand that? Together, the three of us will make this work." I say.

She stares at me, tears in her eyes. I tug on her, drawing her into me with a gentle kiss.

"We love you," I murmur against her lips. "Let us remind you."

There's a whisper of movement, and Luca circles behind her until she's pressed between us. I look up, watching as he nips at her neck, and she sways. "Come to bed, lovely girl."

There is a moment of hesitation, and then she nods. Luca's grip, on her hips, tightens momentarily, and then he releases her. "Get her undressed, English."

I smile, lazily, and step away from her enough to catch the hem of her sweater, tugging it up over her head. The thin silk cami she's wearing trembles as she waits, and I slip my fingertips under it teasingly, playing over the sensitive skin on her belly. Luca makes an impatient noise in the back of his throat, and I grin, lifting it off smoothly. Then I crouch down, unbuttoning her jeans and peeling them down her legs. She wavers when I lift her foot to tug the pants off each leg, but Luca holds her steady.

I sit back on my heels, and Luca gives me a cocky smile. "She's not naked."

"Neither are you," I shoot back. He laughs, and he strips without fanfare. Luca doesn't need fanfare.

He tugs Megan to the bed and sprawls across it, settling her over him.

"Join us, Asher," she whispers. It's more invitation than I need. Dark fingers skim over her hips, cupping her breasts, and she squirms. Luca catches one ankle with his foot, pinning it.

Ah. That's his game.

She watches me as I pull my t-shirt off and slip my jeans down, her eyes hot and hungry as I crawl up the bed toward them. Luca pinches slightly, and she whimpers, bucking as much as she can in his embrace.

"So pretty," I murmur, staring at them.

"She's ready for you," he says, one hand dropping to brush over the green scrap of silk she's calling panties. I follow the motion. My cock jerks.

I catch her panties by one side and jerk, hard. Megan whimpers, and I slip a finger through her folds. She arches against me, and I take a grip on her free leg, holding her still as I drop my head and lick her.

Luca

Megan is whimpering, a twitching mess of feeling as Asher goes down on her.

"You like that, sweetheart?" I whisper, and she groans. I pinch her nipples, just a hint of pain that jerks her away from the edge of climax. I want her riding that edge—I don't want to shove her over.

"Asher," I grit out, and he looks up at me. His eyes find mine, and there's a moment of wordlessness. Then his wet fingers are stroking over my cock, and I hiss.

"Fuck," Megan gasps. "Asher, don't stop."

I'm going to come a lot faster than I want if she doesn't stop. I shift her just a little, my cock slipping up and easing into her. She whimpers, and I thrust as Asher shifts, sucking at her clit. It's shallow—and she shivers, her body tightening around me.

"You okay, sweetheart?" I whisper.

She nods, frantically. Asher shifts, rolling to his knees and scooting up the bed. "Fuck her, Luca," he says, stroking his cock, his voice hoarse.

She reaches for him, and he slides closer.

I shift my hips, thrusting into her as she works his dick. His words reign down on us, a soft pepper of endearments and curses. She groans as I shove deeper, and Asher hisses.

"I'm close," I warn, and Asher's eyes fly open. Find mine as he bucks once. Twice. Megan screams as he jerks away, her body tightening, and I can't think—the orgasm slams into me, jerking away everything but pure sensation as Megs collapses against me, her body twitching. I roll us to the side, and Asher eases into her. She groans, a low, pleased noise.

"Shhh," he murmurs. I stroke her hair watching as he fucks her with a lazy precision, until she whimpers and shivers, gasping out loud while her hands search frantically for us.

Finally, finally, he slips free of her. I curl around her as he pads to the bathroom and gets rid of the condom. Comes back and cleans her gently before tossing the towel to me.

"What times it?" Megan mutters, her voice a sleepy slur.

"Not time to get ready, babe. Close your eyes." I hit the lights and curl against her. On the other side, Asher stretches out on his back, Megan resting against his shoulder.

There are still things to work out—Kevin and Nik and the public to worry about. But as I lie in bed with them, I'm not worried about it. Or even thinking about it. All that matters is that we're together, and we're willing to work for each other. For the first time since Dylan, falling asleep with two other people doesn't make me feel sad or guilty.

Megan's phone chirps from the desk, and I lift my head to glance in its direction. She protests with a whimper, tugging me toward her, and I go, slipping a hand over her waist as we give in to sleep.

Acknowledgements

It's been a while since we ventured to Branton, and I wanted to thank the people who helped make sure we *did* get back.

Chanteé, for tolerating my romance (without dead bodies). And for putting up with me when I tossed the first outline. And the second. And third. And for cheering me on when I *finally* figured out Luca's story. You're the best.

To Bri for loving the boys and keeping me moving and answering totally inappropriate questions.

Special thanks goes to my amazing editor Rachel, who makes the words make sense—any typos or grammar issues are all on me.

To Mel, who read my synopsis and said, 'This is different' and when I said it tied back, gave me a perfect cover, one that embraces the different, and still ties back.

A huge pile of hugs and chocolate to KP and Jessica of InkSlinger, because seriously? Y'all are the best. And didn't even bat an eye when I said I was writing a NA with a threesome.

Thanks to Hailey and Tim, for watching the kids and helping keep my house functioning when I was buried in deadline.

Branton would be a sad lonely place without the bloggers and fans, and a special thank you goes to all of you for loving this University as much as I do.

And last on the list, but first in my heart—my family. Thanks for putting up with my crazy.

www.ingramcontent.com/pod-product-compliance
Lightning Source LLC
Chambersburg PA
CBHW060053150626
46556CB00017BA/170